NO OTHER LOVE

No Other Love

Myrna Diffey

THORNDIKE
CHIVERS

This Large Print edition is published by Thorndike Press, Waterville, Maine, USA and by BBC Audiobooks Ltd, Bath, England.

Thorndike Press is an imprint of Thomson Gale, a part of The Thomson Corporation.

Thorndike is a trademark and used herein under license.

The text of this Large Print edition is unabridged.

Other aspects of the book may vary from the original edition.

Set in 16 pt. Plantin.

LIBRARY OF CONGRESS CATALOGING-IN-PUBLICATION DATA

Diffey, Myrna.
  No other love / by Myrna Diffey.
    p. cm.
  ISBN-13: 978-0-7862-9572-2 (lg. print : alk. paper)
  ISBN-10: 0-7862-9572-4 (lg. print : alk. paper)
  1. Large type books. I. Title.
  PR6054.I376N6 2007
  813'.6—dc22   2007004537

BRITISH LIBRARY CATALOGUING-IN-PUBLICATION DATA AVAILABLE

Published in 2007 in the U.S. by arrangement with Robert Hale Limited.
Published in 2007 in the U.K. by arrangement with Robert Hale Limited.

U.K. Hardcover: 978 1 405 64092 3 (Chivers Large Print)
U.K. Softcover: 978 1 405 64093 0 (Camden Large Print)

Printed and bound in Great Britain by Antony Rowe Ltd, Chippenham, Wiltshire

10 9 8 7 6 5 4 3 2 1

No Other Love

Tel. 6269324/5

ONE

Even after she had closed the drawer she'd been tidying, Grant's photo still lay, face upwards, where she had put it on a nearby table.

Louise looked at it, again. 'All my love, always. Grant.'

What a lot had happened since he'd given her that photo. Grant had proposed . . . she had turned him down . . . and in the end she had lost him to a girl named Annabel, which had served her right, she supposed.

A foolish move? She blamed her parents for that: Julia and Howard, whose stormy marriage had given her an unhappy childhood. Not for me! she had vowed, when other girls became engaged; she knew too well what marriage could bring. But Grant had loved her, no mistake about that and several girls, Marian Taylor for one, had been openly jealous of her. Marian had even tried to get Grant herself, after which —

because of lost face when she'd failed? — she had never been other than aloof with Louise, even though they'd lived near to each other.

Of all the set in which they'd moved, Marian and Louise were the only two still single; everyone else had married. There had been several men, of course — for Louise anyway — but always she had broken the moment they had wanted things serious. She had no regrets. If she was sometimes lonely, at least she was safe, she would think.

When the telephone rang, she put the photo away, resisting the temptation to kiss Grant's mouth as if saying goodbye to him, again. A man's voice asked: "Is that Millstead 507? And are you Mr, Mrs, or Miss Mackenzie who runs a Portraits of Pets Service?"

Louise said, yes, and Miss Mackenzie was the name; explaining that her portraits were painted from photos, which must be colour prints, of course, unless she could see the pet.

Well, he would want to view some of her work first, he said, so could he bring a photograph and go from there? He could call that evening, if convenient.

Amazing how people who left off at five expected those who ran a private concern to be open at all hours! But never mind, all clients were welcome. Having given him her full address, Louise asked: "Would six o'clock be all right?"

"Yes, fine. I'm not far from Millstead," he said, "no distance at all in a car. I can find you quite easily, I take it?"

"You can't miss the house," Louise told him. And because this was important, was careful to stress that she didn't, herself, live at Robins Rest, but in the granny annexe attached. "Up four steps, a dolls' house of a place, half covered with ivy," she explained.

Louise loved her little home. Just a sitting room, kitchen, bedroom en suite, and a workroom where she could paint. That was all and as much as she wanted. Eleanor Russell, who owned Robins Rest, had insisted she also had a small strip of garden. "Just to put a frill around the place!" It was two years now since Louise had moved in. She'd spent her twenty second birthday arranging her possessions; and on that same day her father had married Gail, who was young enough to be his daughter.

He'd been so sure no one would approve of the union that the wedding had been strictly private. Louise's mother had already found a second husband, having broken up a marriage to get the wealthy Bernard

Driscoll, never mind his wife's feelings on the subject. "See the name Mackenzie in every divorce list," Louise had told Eleanor, as bitter as she'd sounded; but Eleanor, who was Julia's dearest friend, kept a still tongue and just smiled.

Four years had passed since Julia and Howard had stormed out of each other's lives; Louise had left the house with them. A lifetime of enduring their constant quarrels had left her with no wish to live with either; she couldn't even like them, as she should. But digs had proved expensive and not really her thing; she'd been glad when Eleanor had offered her the annexe which, surprisingly, had seemed more like home than the house in which she'd been reared.

Now, as Louise replaced the phone, Eleanor herself arrived. "Marian's looking in, this evening," she said. "I thought I'd better warn you, dear." Her laugh as she spoke was apologetic. "Well, you're not exactly buddies are you?" she remarked. "Everyone knows that, don't they?"

Louise tried to smile. It seemed typical of life that fate should guide Marian to Bury St Edmunds after none of them had seen her for months. And typical of Eleanor that, while shopping in Bury, she must bump into this girl. Anyone else might have left it at that, but not Eleanor Russell. By giving Marian her telephone number and details as to how Robins Rest could be reached, she had brought this girl back into their lives, once more, whether they wanted her or didn't.

"Though in any case," Louise said, "I've a visitor, myself, this evening. A client, that is to say." She pushed her light brown hair away from her forehead, looking at Eleanor from clear hazel eyes, unaware how attractive she was. "Wouldn't you think," she went on, "that Marian could forgive me after all this time? I didn't take Grant away from her, you know. I couldn't help it if he took a fancy to me. Truthfully, I never encouraged him."

"A pity you didn't," Eleanor replied. "Quite apart from the very obvious fact that Grant's bound to make quite a name for himself, we all thought him a very nice fellow. But then, just as we were thinking there'd be wedding bells ringing, you had to give him the brush-off, you silly girl!"

Louise shrugged. Not to anyone in the world would she admit she'd been a fool to turn Grant down; pride would not permit that. Occasionally, in private, she would allow the admission; but then she'd cancel it out, asking herself how could she regret

11

breaking with Grant when she was sworn to stay clear of marriage? She had gone to his wedding, kissed the lovely Annabel, but had done no more than congratulate Grant. The kisses to which he and she had been accustomed couldn't be reduced to a mere peck, and Grant must have known that was so. Since his marriage, she had seen nothing of him; but someone said he was a fully fledged solicitor, now, which didn't surprise Louise.

No particular success in her own life, as yet; though she was satisfied with what she had. There'd been that small annuity her grandfather had left her, which just about kept the wolf from the door; for the rest, she earned a reasonable income designing posters and — the job she liked most — her Portraits of Pets Service.

Eleanor gone, Louise snatched a quick meal before arranging a few sample portraits in a neat semi-circle on the table. She tidied her room because she hated disorder; besides, a good impression paid off. It might be recognised that most artists lived in chaos; but where the portrait of a prized cat or dog was involved, people liked to feel the work was carried out in more exclusive surroundings.

Her client arrived punctually at six. He

12

had given his name, but somehow she had missed it. Now, he said it again. "Adrian Pryce. I rang you earlier about a protrait of my dog."

Louise nodded. "Do come in . . ." Medium to tall, with thick black hair, he had penetrating eyes, dark as coals, and a deep cleft in his chin. Said to denote a flirt, so people said; though there was nothing of that in this man's manner as he stood looking at Louise. Even his smile was no more than polite as he said: "What a charming place this is! Even a nice little garden to yourself — and quite separate from the house, I take it?"

"Separate, but attached," Louise confirmed, and smiled as she thought of the panic button which Eleanor had had installed. "Well, you never know," she had said, sternly; though what Eleanor, widowed with no man in the house — even Eleanor assisted by Kim the maid — could do in the event of a sudden attack, Louise couldn't imagine.

Still, there it was, staring at her from the wall; and as Eleanor had said, one never knew, though no one could have looked less like a villain than this man who had just been admitted. Seated, he produced a photograph which he handed, smiling, to Louise.

"Oh, yes, a really beautiful labrador," she said. It was a recognised necessity that pets must be praised; though mostly, and this was another such occasion, it was easy to be sincere.

"And the photograph's okay?"

"Yes, very good and clear. What is your dog's name?" she asked.

"Fritz. Unhappily, he's dead, now. He was eight years old when this was taken. I do have other photos," Pryce volunteered. "I should have brought one of just his head and shoulders, which gives a better idea of his expression. I could bring that tomorrow, if you like?"

"Or you could post it to me," Louise suggested.

"No . . ." He shook his head. "I'd rather bring it, myself. Anything that's lost now, can't be replaced, and I was fond of the old fellow. Sorry if that sounds sentimental, Miss Mackenzie, but a dog really *can* steal one's heart."

"If you knew how some clients go on about their pets, you wouldn't apologise," Louise assured him. "Though it's nice that people do love their animals." Rising, she turned towards the portraits on the table.

"You wanted to see some of my work? I've purposely put dogs on view, nothing else, so that you can see what I've done."

Pryce looked at them and gave a pleased whistle. "Well, yes, they're super," he exclaimed. "Even better than I'd expected."

"Well, thank you . . ." This was where the interview should end, because Pryce was satisfied with her terms and obviously admired her work. But now he had dropped into his chair again, and Louise could only do the same. From dogs they went to films, to music, to books, while the minutes ticked on through an hour and a half. She'd have to offer him a drink soon, Louise thought, except she hoped he would not stay that long.

Though in many ways she found him a likeable companion, she decided against offering him a drink. That would simply be encouraging him to stay and she didn't want him there until midnight.

One quick glance at her watch brought him to his feet. "I'm keeping you," he said, embarrassed. "But I've enjoyed my visit; I could happily have stayed all evening." She made no comment and he continued, smiling at her, "And a nice surprise to find, not a drab little office with some hard business type seated at a desk, but a charming little

15

house and an equally charming girl. This is certainly my lucky night!"

Louise laughed. "No reduction for flattery."

"Oh, but I mean it," he protested. "Look, won't you call me Adrian? I know we've only just met, but already I feel we're friends."

Louise hesitated. Business was business. Clients came and went and it was very seldom she saw any of them more than twice, so did it matter if for once she bent the rules and called one by his Christian name? The cleft in this man's chin — what was he, thirty five? — didn't seem to have been put there for nothing, after all. But: "Okay, Adrian," she answered.

He was smiling again. "I'll bring the other photo over, then," he promised Louise. "You can look at both and decide which is best."

Watching him leave, her restless mind insisted on comparing him with Grant Sullivan. Grant, her first love . . . He'd lain his heart at her feet; there'd never be another Grant in her life. She had known within days that she'd been mad to turn him down, because she *had* been in love with him. A pity she had found his photo, that day. A pity, in a way, that she had kept it all this time; though even without his picture to remind her, she knew she could never have forgotten him.

And now this man. A stranger, yet — quoting himself — already they had found themselves friends. And in a way, Louise was pleased, for until that evening she hadn't realised how lonely she was. Too soon to see him as a second chance to love; for all she knew, he was married with children. Though in any case, would she *want* to take things further? Her parents' marriage, still prominent in her mind, persisted as a warning to her.

She saw Marian arrive and within half an hour Eleanor and this girl were tapping at the door: Eleanor, rolling her eyes as they entered, knowing they were not really welcome.

"We're not staying," she began, as if to comfort Louise, "but Marian wanted to see your little home. Also, she has some news of her own, haven't you, dear?" she prompted.

What news? An engagement? No, nothing so romantic. Marian laughed, as if she thought her news trivial. "Only that I've bought a bungalow near Bury," she said, marvelling at Eleanor's interest. "Hardly exciting, is it?"

"But nice, though." Louise kept her voice bright. A pity Eleanor had got involved with this girl when she had no reason to do so. She made her home open house to everyone she met, and naturally they all took advantage of this and were forever popping in and out. Louise turned to Marian. "How many rooms? And have you a nice garden?"

But she couldn't fox Marian any more than Marian had Louise fooled. They were being polite, nothing more. However hard they tried nothing they did could return them to the footing on which they had been before Grant had come into their lives. Yet had they ever been all that close? Louise queried. They'd been part of a set; but for most of the time Marian had seemed to dislike her.

Now, she said: "The garden's small, which suits me nicely since I've never had green fingers. I've six rooms in all — seven, if one counts the sun room." As she spoke, she looked around, surveying Louise's lounge and said, "God, I couldn't live in this! Who was it built for, a midget? Sorry!" Marian gave a don't-care laugh. "But it really *is* tiny, isn't it?"

"Really?" Louise lifted both eyebrows. "To me, the size is part of its charm." She added, purposely changing he subject:

18

"You're working in Bury St Edmunds, then? Have you been there long?"

Marian shrugged. It always seemed to Louise that Marian purposely resorted to this gesture to let people know how little they mattered to her. "Like yourself, I wanted a change," she said. "So when I saw this advert for a qualified dispenser — and quite a big chemist shop at that — I couldn't resist applying."

Before Louise could answer, she added, impatiently now: "I'm sorry, I'll have to get out of this place! It reminds me of the time I got locked in a loo. I'm not happy in confined spaces . . ."

Nor in my company! Louise judged, correctly, as Marian sidled towards the door. Eleanor looked openly hurt. She was rather proud of this little place she had rented to Louise and had expected Marian to be charmed. Even the furniture — some secondhand, some sanded down and painted by Louise — even this had delighted Eleanor. Really Marian could be most difficult.

After they had left — Eleanor, tall and slim, young for sixty with her flawless complexion, her wide open eyes and fluffy grey hair: Marian, pixie faced, small and blonde — Louise gave a sigh of relief.

Tired, she planned an early night; except

that Marian's bitchy comments made her restless. Or was it finding Grant's photo? She had forgotten how disturbing he could be. Returning to her bedroom, she looked at the photo, and on an impulse stood it on her bedside table. From there, Grant could smile at her across the years . . .

Could smile and turn her heart clean over.

Two

Adrian swung his Datsun into the drive, parked it against the laurel hedge as far as he could from Eleanor's house, then rang Louise's bell at the annexe.

"I see you have a name plate for your house," he said, amused.

"That's right . . ." Louise looked at it and smiled. "That's to stop people from bothering Mrs Russell. She isn't a fusspot, far from it, but why have her disturbed when a name plate is all that is needed?"

"I didn't see it when I called yesterday, that's all."

"No, it only went up today." Louise had painted and fixed it, herself: soft brown lettering edged with gilt on a slither of wood cut from a tree which Eleanor's gardener and young Brock Seymour had felled a year or so back.

They went indoors and she said, remembering why he'd come: "You've brought the photo, I hope?"

"Yes, I have — and here it is, Louise. You don't mind if I call you Louise?" Adrian asked.

The second photo was nothing like as good as the first; Louise felt he had brought it more as an excuse than in an effort to get a good likeness.

"I'll stick to the original, I think," she told him.

"Okay, I'll leave that to you." He retrieved the second photo which he pushed into his wallet. "Pretty busy are you?" he asked.

"Fairly, yes." She would never be over-loaded, not in her line of business, nor would she wish to be. So long as she made a reasonable living, enough to supplement the income she received, then that did her nicely.

They began to talk, Adrian explaining that his firm dealt in agricultural machinery; that he was part of the office staff. It could make him feel quite excited, he admitted, to see those big mechanical giants lined up; the great combines, in particular, really did something to him.

Louise wanted to say that though today's machinery had certainly changed things for the better; yet, viewed from a sentimental angle, what a lot of pageantry had gone out with these improvements. Events like harvest suppers, one read about . . . everyone working in the fields by moonlight. It all needed to go, but what a pity.

All remarks she might well have made to Grant; but not to this man who now said, shyly — shyly and a little prematurely, in her view: "Do you know, I like you very much, Louise! I like you more and more, every minute . . ."

"Well, let's see if you like my coffee," she said, refusing him any further moves along that line. "And by the way, I'd better have your telephone number. I can ring you, then, when I've finished Fritz's portrait."

Adrian handed her his card which she put to one side. "That will mostly find me," he said. "If I'm out, someone will take a message." He watched her move towards the door. "May I join you?" he asked. And Louise saw no alternative, except to comply, though she would rather he had stayed put. But now there he was, getting in her way, still watching her from eyes that were seeking, admiring . . .

A little *too* admiring, she decided, frowning. He was making her embarrassed, now.

Taking the tray from her hands, he said: "I'm sticking my neck out, saying this, but I enjoy coming here, Louise. If I look in now and then, it's not to hassle you, at all; just to have your company," he told her.

A difficult moment. She wasn't certain, yet, how she felt about this man. Already, he'd assumed he could come when he wished; so despite his shy appearance, he wasn't slow in coming forward once he knew what he wanted.

"Well, it's nice to have someone to talk to," he excused. "Don't get me wrong, I'm not short of friends, but most of them don't seem my type. I'm thirty six, which makes me older than you. By what? A good ten years, I'd say. Am I correct?" he asked.

"More or less — I'm twenty four," she supplied.

"That's about what I thought you would be. And a bachelor girl, too, since I don't see any ring — which rather surprises me," he said. "However, that being the case, Louise, you're not going to blame me if I *do* put in a plea to see you now and then, are you?"

"What's now and then?" she wanted to know.

"Just as often as you'll let me," he answered. "Yes, of course you have other friends, other commitments, so I musn't intrude too often." He set the tray down on the coffee table. "Only tell me you'll be pleased to see me. Perhaps you'll allow me to take you out, some time? You will, won't you?" he coaxed.

"I'll see what I can fix . . ." She was careful to sound pleased, not liking to hurt his feelings. "Ask me a little later, will you?"

She liked Adrian. There were times, and this was one such patch, when she knew she would like a man's company. If she broke when things threatened to become serious, she was only being honest she'd argue.

Adrian stayed two hours. When he said goodnight, Louise half expected he would want to kiss her, then was glad that after all he didn't.

She watched his Datsun pull away into the Summer night, and almost at once her eye was caught by something that looked like the figure of a man dodging between the shadows. It couldn't be, of course, Louise told herself. Surely, she was just imagining things? If there *had* been a person, he had gone now; though why would he be there, anyway? More than likely, it was some lad from the village. Or Brock Seymour, maybe? For a while, Brock had worked at Robins Rest as a not very competent under-gardener, and rumour had it he was rather keen on Kim.

Louise paused, glancing around, listening

for the rustle of movements; but the shrubs and trees edging the garden were still as sentries on guard. She hadn't the courage to make a search; best to write it off as a trick of the mind, before she frightened herself.

Closing the door, she let her thoughts turn to Adrian. He was gone; yet something of himself seemed left behind. She imagined he would make a persistent suitor: one good reason why he should not be encouraged, unless she was prepared to be loved. Best to let things ride, she told herself. Time enough, later, for decisions.

The following evening was all her own. Adrian had phoned expressing disappointment that he wasn't able to get along — quite unaware that, since Louise was busy, she preferred to be free from visitors.

She had spent her afternoon designing a poster for the local Methodists' Summer Fair — free, because one couldn't charge a church. Now, she was glad to sit out of doors in what Eleanor, who could sometimes brood a little, called the 'sad of the day'. Louise loved the stillness of a garden losing colour as the first shadows wrapped it around.

Sitting there, she knew herself to be lucky.

When one thought of the very ordinary surroundings in which the majority of people lived, it was as well to realise that to spend one's life in a charming Suffolk village with fields all around and a great expanse of Constable sky overhead, was nothing short of a privilege.

Kim came out to see what Louise was at, sitting on the steps at this time of day, even eating her supper out of doors. A sandy haired girl with a dumpy figure and — to quote the gardener — as thick as two sitcks, Kim was good hearted and hard working; Eleanor considered her a treasure.

"You mind them midges don't get at you, Miss," she told Louise, gently scolding. "It's harvest time, don't forget. I got sitting on the grass, once, with a boy and me backside got smothered with bites."

"Was that Brock you were with when the midges bit you?"

"No, I don't like Brock," Kim replied. "When he used to work here, I kept indoors. Cheeky thing, he tried to kiss me, once. 'That's only for courting', I told him."

Louise laughed. "And did that put him in his place?"

"It takes more'n that to slap Brock down," Kim said. She set her mouth in a prim straight line. "I don't want no boys, yet," she told Louise. "I'd rather stay with Mrs Russell."

"Well, you certainly have a very good job . . ." Louise felt her forehead pucker. *Was* that Brock she had seen among the shrubs? There wouldn't be much point in his hanging around if Kim wasn't interested in him; in which case someone else had been there. She wasn't going to make an issue of it, yet for all that she felt perplexed. But she let the subject go as Eleanor appeared.

"I'm full of apologies," she began. "I forgot to deliver a message to you. That was very remiss of me, wasn't it?"

"Depends on the message." Louise shot her a grin.

"I should have remembered," she was told. "Actually, this came while you were out shopping. Your mother phoned, and in the course of our little ten minute chat she said she wondered if you'd like a day at Braintree, preferably this coming Sunday? She and Bernard thought it would be nice to see you again. You could borrow my car," Eleanor offered. "I shan't be wanting it, myself."

"Thank you, Eleanor . . ." Did a sigh escape? It seemed wrong that she had to be winkled out like this, instead of going of her own accord. It wasn't that she held anything against her mother, now. Just that they had never been very close — and the fact that it embarrassed her to be with Bernard.

But she must go. Of course she must, she owned; just as she must sometimes visit her father in order not to lose contact. A strange reason: it ought to have been that she visited her parents out of affection — except they'd never taught her to love them. But at least they were satisfied — delighted, in fact! — with the partners they'd acquired. Was she expected to rejoice with them? They had apparently forgotten the endless rows which had sent their small daughter to cower in the garden, or had made her tremble in bed. Had forgotten the love affairs each had as proof that they could easily find someone else — no matter that Louise would fret herself sick, wondering how she stood in all this.

She had lived through the whole of her adolescence waiting for the final break to come; and the fact that her parents had remained together until she was almost out of her teens, hadn't made her any more secure. She'd never told them how she'd missed the family closeness which other youngsters seemed privileged to enjoy.

But all that must be left to slide away into the past. She was twenty four, now, and there was nothing to be gained by fretting over something which couldn't be altered; far better to put it all from her mind before bitterness enveloped her again.

Rising, Louise stretched the stiffness from her limbs and let her gaze reach out to the thick-growing shrubs, eyes and brain alert as she stood there. There was no one around, she was sure of that. Perhaps there had been no one the previous night; yet her certainty that she had not been mistaken made her feel uneasy. She would not tell Eleanor. It could have been someone who'd been taken short, as one of her grandmothers used to say; some people did have that weakness.

Adrian came the next evening. Watching him arrive, Louise was surprised how pleased she was to see him: even realised, with further surprise, that she had actually missed this man.

And: "Nice to be with you, again," he said, echoing her own feelings. "But before we go any further, Louise — I'm after a date this coming weekend. How about Sunday — yes?"

Louise couldn't manage Sunday; she'd already phoned her mother and the whole day was filled, she explained. "Though I could make it Monday," she told him.

"Fair enough, Monday it shall be," he said. "We'll have a really nice evening, shall we? Go somewhere super! I'll call for you at seven, okay?"

She risked a question which refused to remain unasked:

"You're sure your wife wouldn't mind?"

Adrian's face straightened. For one tense moment, Louise was sure he was angry and offended; but he flicked the scowl away, saying bluntly: "Do you think I'd dare risk taking you out if I had a wife in the background? I wouldn't even suggest it in fun."

"I'm sorry . . . I had to be certain, that's all."

"Well, put it from your mind," he told her. "No wife, I promise you; and in case you are thinking that Monday will be the end of the story, let me warn you here and now that it's only the beginning, Louise."

She wasn't sure she wanted him to call too often. It was nice to invite people in when it suited; but not to be invaded evening after evening, she would find that overwhelming. The truth was, however nice the person, she didn't want anyone to be too possessive — only she couldn't say this to Adrian.

Somehow, she managed to dodge answer-

31

ing; even persuaded a change of mood by playing some of her tapes. When at last she looked at the watch on her wrist, the hands had flown to eleven o'clock.

"I'm afraid I have to turn you out, now," she said. "I've a busy day ahead of me, tomorrow."

That was a fib, but he accepted the statement, even though he said, his voice persuasive: "Do I truly have to go? Must I?"

"Yes, I'm sorry, but you do."

"I see . . ." The scowl was back; Adrian even looked sulky, she decided. "I'll leave coming until Monday, then," he said. "I'm going to miss you — you know that, don't you?"

"I don't think so," she smiled. "If you *do* miss me, I'm a lot more dynamic than I thought."

"You're that, all right," he said. At the door, he paused. Took her tenderly into his embrace. She felt his lips brush her mouth, once . . . twice . . . before pressing down hard in a long searching kiss, leaving them both breathless. Even then, he didn't leave her; but, tilting her chin, looked into her eyes, saying quietly: "Now you know . . . if you needed me to tell you."

She wouldn't argue, nor take him seriously, she vowed; yet watching him drive away into the night, still aware of his kisses, excited by them, Louise knew too well how easy it would be to lose her heart to Adrian.

Her thoughts stayed trained on Julia and Howard; and now she wondered if, perhaps, she had judged them too harshly? Though surely she also had a right of opinion? She didn't *have* to approve of her parents. Were she to marry, she would want things to last.

Though what was wrong with falling in love? Louise smiled at the question. Almost everyone did, sooner or later, so why not herself, with them?

Even so, it couldn't be Adrian — or could it? Feeling as she did that particular evening, there was no saying what might happen.

Louise closed the door and locked it for the night. No, she didn't think she'd get that far — not yet; she preferred to take things more slowly. Yet he wasn't someone she could easily forget; and that night, she didn't want to forget him.

THREE

Eleanor's loan of her new Mini solved all problems of travelling and got Louise to Braintree in time for mid-morning coffee.

Bernard, in shorts and open necked shirt, gold locket lost in the fuzz on his chest, was busying himself putting chairs and a table for the three of them to use on the patio. He had acquired a tan and had allowed his hair to grow long enough to touch his collar at the back; and with his tinted glasses and gold-toothed smile was so much a made-to-measure husband for Julia that Louise marvelled she had ever even looked Howard's way.

Not that Howard could be condemned as anything but smart; just that he preferred the conventional. He would no more have been seen with bare legs and shorts, let alone wear a locket around his neck, than he'd have gone through Piccadilly in pyjamas. The two men could hardly have been more different, just as Julia and Gail, separated as they were by very nearly twenty years, bore no resemblance to each other. Gail, a slim little elfin thing: Julia, plumply blonde and feminine to an extreme. Louise looked at her mother, now pouring coffee, and decided she had done very well for herself to get exactly the husband she wanted.

Julia wanted to know how Eleanor was. "We're surprised she never married again," Bernard said. "Edwin wouldn't have wanted her to stay a widow, he wes never a selfish man . . ." And what had Louise been up to? he asked. Julia adding: "We don't hear much from you, these days. This is your first visit for ages — and then we had to *ask* you to come!"

Louise answered all their questions, made suitable replies, explained that the almost new Mini in the drive belonged to Eleanor Russell. She didn't envy these two their beautiful home, their endless leisure and the banking account from which they could draw ad lib. Home to Louise was her little granny annexe with pansies and marigolds in her own strip of garden, and the long view of cornfields from the windows. She couldn't have held a dinner, or cocktail party, even had she known the sort of people to invite; there were only chairs for four, anyway. As for travelling the world — 'We haven't yet seen Japan!' — well, that was right at the bottom of the list; she was still saving up for a car.

But they made her welcome, Louise acknowledged. Really and genuinely welcome. Julia had gone to town over lunch: Bernard, acting the perfect host, bending over backwards all the time, literally fussing Louise. "You must come more often . . ."

They spent the afternoon relaxing on the patio, the only sounds reaching their ears as they talked being the whirr of a distant mowing machine and laughter from neighbours playing tennis.

Suddenly, Bernard asked, as if prompted from backstage: "Still the sworn bachelor girl, my dear?"

"Maybe," was all she answered.

"Well, you shouldn't still be going it alone," Bernard said. "By now, *someone* should have turned you on enough to send you racing to the altar."

She shrugged, thinking, what a way to put it! "You're more worried than I am," she told him.

Julia crushed her cigarette and sat up to declare: "Well, leave it long enough and you'll end on the shelf. The years soon pass, you know." Her eyes were on her daughter. "Is there no one at all?" Playful though she sounded, the question was a feeler, and an irritating feeler at that. Later on, Julia would want a grandchild or two; and unless Louise shed all this bachelor girl rot, it was no use dreaming about them.

Though there was more to it than that, Louise decided. Someone had been talking. Eleanor? Who else? News of Adrian's visits had gone on ahead; and now Julia's beautifully shaped nose was sniffing the air for more news.

Though there wasn't much point in her doing that, for what was there to say about Adrian? He wasn't even a friend in the true sense, and certainly not Louise's lover. Agreed, he'd be taking her out the next evening and, yes, his visits to the annexe had been lengthy; but that hardly made him her up and coming spouse, did it?

Julia sighed. She let the subject drop; Louise came so seldom, it would be a pity to have the conversation take an awkward turn and perhaps upset the girl. Bernard, too, sensed the time had come to move on to something more tactful; though in any case, the sound of a car's arrival had brought him swiftly to his feet.

Julia's sigh sharpened to a hissed: "Blast!

Now who can *that* be?" she snapped. "Not a soul has looked in the whole week; and then today, when we've managed to get you to ourselves, somebody has to call!" She watched Bernard disappear into the house. "A pity he did that," she told Louise. "He should have stayed put, not gone to the door; though whoever it is might have come to the side. We must have a bolt put on the gate . . ."

Bernard was back. He looked faintly embarrassed. "Er-um, Julia . . ." His eyes turned pleadingly to his wife. "A nice surprise!" He seemed playing for time. "After all this time, here's Grant suddenly arrived . . ."

Julia jumped like someone who'd been sprayed with cold water. Louise somehow managed to stay calm; in a way, she felt slightly stunned. But she turned in her chair to meet Grant's eyes, feeling warmed by the smile he flashed her.

There he stood, the only man she had ever loved, looking not at Julia or Bernard, now, but straight into her own hazel eyes, as if this were the purpose of his visit.

"Grant!" Julia squealed; and remembering her presence, he promptly gave her a kiss. This done, he put another on Louise's cheek before shaking hands with them both.

His face was unaltered, even though he looked strained, like a man who for too long had worked too hard; yet still the Grant they had known. His dark chestnut hair, with its persistence to curl despite the fact that it was kept fairly short — that, and the healthy texture of his skin seemed to set off the well-cut safari suit and the blue-grey of his eyes.

He was not a handsome man. Good looking, perhaps, and endowed with his own sort of rugged features which made people look at him more than once and having done so, never to forget him. The whole six foot two of him was at last persuaded to take Bernard's chair while another was fetched; his arrival seemed to complete the party — made the four of them become two pairs.

"Well, this *is* nice!" You would never have thought Julia had earlier blasted his arrival. "And you're looking fine, Grant," she told him.

"So are you . . . and you!" he said, including Louise. Did his eyes rest upon her just a fraction longer than when he had addressed Julia? She mustn't imagine things, must she? This was Grant being courteous, nothing more, because of course he belonged to Annabel, now; and she, Louise Mackenzie, had schooled herself to accept that he had gone from her life. She had had every chance, but had thrown them away — not without a great many protests from Grant who had loved her almost to distraction. She had hurt him and fate had hit back at her, she owned, by giving her four long lonely years . . .

Looking at him, now, she recalled the moment when they had first met each other. She'd been twenty, still shattered by her parents' divorce: Grant, just four years older. For a time they had been no more than friends; with Marian always there, doing her damnedest to get herself included wherever they went, and making no secret of the fact that she'd wanted Grant for herself.

But she had reckoned without his grim determination to get the girl who had really won his heart; and in the end, tactfully or otherwise, Grant had succeeded in shedding Marian and had taken Louise as his sweetheart.

Annabel had also been around. Shy, sweet Annabel, forever in the background, like some beautiful wallflower, waiting. She hadn't pushed, as Marian Taylor had; but she had always been there, and when Louise broke Grant's heart who but Annabel could pick up the pieces.

Had their love affair been as wonderful as the one she herself had known with Grant? Louise wondered. Even now, she marvelled she had ever found the strength to bring things to an end, as she had. Not that Grant had been easy. Having boasted all round that he fully intended marrying Louise, he found having to lose hard to take, and for weeks had refused to give in.

"Don't regard your parents as being typical," he had said. "Marriage needn't be like that. Ours needn't! Ours *wouldn't* be like that! For God's sake, why should it be, Louise?"

But she wouldn't believe he could be so certain, with the result that she had lost him to Annabel; and chance what blame she put upon her parents, she could really only turn it upon herself, because who else had sent Grant packing?

Lucky, lucky Annabel who had won Grant's love! Someone should ask after her, Louise thought. But somehow she couldn't, and neither Julia nor Bernard were taking any chances on the subject. They weren't going to mention the name of this girl who had robbed them of Grant as a son-in-law.

Grant wasn't mentioning Annabel, either. He had been on his way back through Suffolk, he explained; and having found their

41

address on an old Christmas card, had decided to call since he had almost to pass their door. He paused, as if meaning to add something else; but instead went on to say he was doing quite well and had entered a partnership, now. "Four of us, all of varying ages, which to me makes an ideal firm. I've been using the weekend finalising matters and getting my office as I want it."

"You're right in the law game, now, then," Bernard asked, using his man-of-the-world tone of voice. "Any murderers come your way, yet?"

Grant let a grin accompany his answer. "Professional etiquette, or however you like to word it, doesn't permit me to say."

"Until you put it in your autobiography," Julia said. "Memoirs of a famous lawyer . . ."

They all laughed, more from good manners than amusement; Grant's smile, directed at Louise, now, made it hard not to love him, again. "And how are you getting on?" he wanted to know. "Are you living here, in Braintree?"

"Not Louise, she's a country lass," Bernard said. "She's dug in at Millstead, with Eleanor Russell. That's so, eh, my dear?"

Louise wondered why Bernard must answer for her; but she followed what he had already said by explaining to Grant that she preferred village life.

"Well, you don't need me to say I'm with you there," he said; and she recalled that once — what an age ago that seemed! — they had loved exploring villages. They had photographed timbered and thatched houses, round-towered churches and village signs; and like everything else she did with Grant, it had all been tremendous fun.

"You'll stay to tea?" Julia asked in her best hostess voice.

"Actually, I'd hoped to hear the kettle whistling when I turned into your drive," he said, fooling. "After all, it *was* four o'clock!"

"Then we'd better get cracking," Julia laughed. "Bernard, you can keep Grant amused while I grab Louise to help me in the kitchen."

As Louise rose, Grant looked up at the girl. "Nice to see you, again," he murmured.

"And nice to see you . . ." She dodged his feet and followed Julia indoors. It surprised her how shaken she was at this moment: shaken and miserable, as well. No matter that Grant was a married man, his voice bridging the lonely years had made Louise want him back again as she would never have believed possible.

"Well, *that* was a surprise!" Julia remarked. "What a lucky thing I got tea ready before hand. Just a matter of putting things out on plates; the trolley is already laid."

Louise felt in a whirl: part of her wanting to speak about Grant, if only for the pleasure of saying his name: part of her dreading what Julia might say, since Grant had been her choice for Louise.

Not that anyone had known why she had given Grant up, nor how deeply she'd regretted her folly. "Just one of those things," was all she'd let herself say . . . and had fooled herself that she had meant it.

Unaware of her thoughts, Julia said: "My God, what a man he is! There's something about Grant — I've never quite known what! — but I've always felt cheated that I couldn't have had him for my only son-in-law."

"Why cheated?" Louise wanted to know.

"My dear, I've just told you, haven't I?" Julia busied herself, arranging meringues. "I would have liked him for a son-in-law. What a marvellous father he'd have made for my grandchildren — the ones I don't ever look like having, now! Though that's *your* fault, of course. And Bernard's childless," she complained, pouting, "so I can't have any step grandchildren, either! Then you ask me why I feel cheated . . ."

Teatime, always a sociable meal, passed

44

pleasantly and smoothly enough. They talked about the drought which still persisted, though there were rumours that there might be a few thundery showers: about the indoor swimming pool Bernard had had installed, and the holiday the Driscolls were taking.

"We haven't yet seen Japan . . ." *Oh, not again!* Louise thought. "But we did get as far as China, last year. Not a country we would want to live in. We wish Louise would come with us on some of our jaunts; it's time she saw a little of the world . . ."

They had just reached the stage when cigarettes were being lighted — the flame of Grant's match quivering slightly as his hand cupped Louise's for a few brief seconds — when Julia observed: "We've all been horribly discourteous! Not one of us has asked after Annabel, Grant! How is she these days? Quite well?"

Grant looked shocked. He blew out the match he'd been holding and studied its black burned tip. "You missed the announcement in the papers, then? I had a feeling you mightn't have seen it . . ." Did he know Louise's heart was hammering for him? For having sensed what he must say, she almost dreaded his next sentence. But he took a quick breath and said, quietly:

45

"Annabel died eleven months ago. She was five months pregnant . . . picked up some sort of virus . . . so unhappily, I lost them both."

FOUR

All the way from Braintree back to Millstead, Louise's thoughts constantly rico-
cheted to Grant, making her restless and
sad. Her mind seemed full of him, now.

Everything had been going exceptionally
well, the four of them pleasantly relaxed, at
last; and then Julia's question coming out
of the blue, throwing them all off balance.

Yes, of course someone needed to mention Annabel, but if only Julia had delayed
enquiring until Grant was leaving the house.
Not that Louise blamed her mother. Julia
was right: they had all been discourteous to
welcome Grant without asking after his wife.

Louise gave a small sigh. As a rule, she
liked this drive: loved the brief colourful
glimpses of fields falling back from the
hedges, like patchwork. Still in Essex, she
felt the landscape soften as Constable
country came out to meet it; but then her
mind was back upon Grant, once more, and

the stammered reply he had given.

'You missed the announcement . . . eleven months ago . . . she was five months pregnant . . . unhappily, I lost them both . . .'

And now that Annabel had died, all Grant's love had gone with her, which accounted for the strained expression in his eyes and those premature 'worry lines'. After he had made that traumatic statement, he had tried to put them at their ease again by speaking of subjects more pleasant, more cheerful; but the discomfort they felt had still shown. Somehow, Grant's arrival had spoiled a day which had gone much better than Louise had expected; yet would she have missed seeing him, whatever the outcome of it all? He had not made any plans to keep in touch. Foolishly, she had hoped he might have done that: not to take up their old relationship, again, but for friendship's sake, she had thought.

Eleanor came out to welcome Louise, eager for all the Braintree news, because news was what Eleanor lived for. No point in omitting Grant's visit; better to get that said while her own expression was hidden in the fast gathering dusk, for Eleanor had very quick eyes.

"Poor Annabel, what a shame!" Eleanor exclaimed. "That could easily have wrecked

Grant's career. I know from my own experience," she said, "what losing a partner can be like . . ." The Mini put away, Eleanor locked the garage. "Come and have a drink," she invited the girl. "Better still, eat supper with me. You've had a long drive home and I bet you won't trouble to get yourself anything, will you?"

Braintree to Millstead hardly constituted what anyone would call a long drive, but she could not snub this woman who had loaned her car and, besides, she was fond of Eleanor.

Once or twice, Eleanor touched upon Grant; but it was growing late, now, and in any case Louise could only tell her very little. He hadn't gone into details concerning his loss, nor said very much about himself, so what was there left to discuss?

"Except," the older woman said, "I hope one day he'll meet somone who will make him happy, again . . ." She let a sharp glance fasten upon Louise, before adding: "By the way, now he's working in Bury, I only hope he'll manage to steer clear of Marian! She's still single, don't forget."

Louise grimaced. She had forgotten Marian; now, suddenly, she felt uneasy. She too hoped that Grant would find happiness, again; but let Marian keep out of the picture, she thought. Grant had never liked this girl, Louise knew that; but people who were lonely could be vulnerable, as well, and Marian could be very tenacious.

Monday brought sunshine to further the drought; it also brought a phone 'call from Adrian Pryce reminding Louise that he was taking her out, that evening. The half dozen kisses which came over the line amused the girl.

She worked hard all day, then took time getting ready: showered, washed her hair and chose a nice dress. When Adrian arrived, he gave a gasp of surprise.

"God, you're beautiful!" he murmured.

His dark eyes took in the whole of her, like someone admiring a painting. "I have to kiss you," he told Louise, "because I want to be with you *every* evening, this week . . . and then again either Saturday, or Sunday."

She laughed, saying: "You'll be lucky!" Though Adrian was fooling, of course, she thought. With those keen dark eyes — perhaps *intense* described them better — it was difficult to determine how serious he was, or even to read his mood.

But: "Let me explain . . ." He still held her in his arms. "I shall probably be working overtime next month. Well, no 'probably' about it — I *shall* be working overtime, which means I shan't get more than two free evenings in the course of each week, for a time. This being so," he kissed her, again, "you can quite understand that, while I can, I want to see you *every* evening . . ."

Things were moving a little too speedily, she thought. The second time this warning had sprung into her brain, she wished Adrian would cool down a little. She didn't want to go through the whole explanation as to why she preferred not to get too involved; . . . although, having met Grant Sullivan again, she had begun to realise that, like it or not, she wasn't quite as determined to remain single as she'd led herself to believe.

Even so, she wasn't parting with too many evenings. Louise still wanted some to herself. Just lately, she had been neglecting her friends, which was never a good idea. She smiled at Adrian as she broke from his embrace. "Will you mind if I say not to book ahead, but to take the evenings as they come?"

"Any special reason for saying this?" he asked.

"Only that I don't care to be tied. Things happen — and then engagements have to be broken. So one day at a time is my maxim."

Adrian took her hand, kissing it fondly before escorting her to where his car was parked. "What happens if I try to date you," he said, "only to find you're already booked up? I'll be out on my ear, then, won't I? So, okay, let me put my claim in first, then I shan't be disappointed."

"We'll see," Louise said. She flicked a glance at Adrian, hoping he wasn't offended, at all — wishing, even though this made no sense, that just for once it could be Grant who was taking her out, who had kissed her and held her close.

Once in the car, they were soon out of Millstead, with Finchingfield not far ahead. "I've booked a table for eight o'clock," Adrian said. "I hope that's all right, is it?"

"Very nice . . ." She felt touched by the effort he had made. Himself nicely groomed: the gift of an orchid lying beautiful and cool in its cellophaned box: even the car freshly polished. They went right out of the district for their meal. "Since we already know our own area," he said, "it makes a change to go somewhere fresh."

"Well, I don't often eat out," Louise confessed, "so any place is still a treat for me, Adrian. I'm sorry if that makes me sound naive, but it really *is* a treat," she said.

"I'm what my mother's second husband calls a country girl; by which, I suspect, he means a country bumpkin!"

"That will be the day," Adrian laughed. "You tell him that someone you know thinks you're gorgeous. Gorgeous and really smart! I'm very proud to be with you, tonight." Twenty minutes later, they reached the place he had chosen. The meal would cost a bomb, Louise decided, but Adrian was enjoying his extravagance. *Well, why not? — you're worth it!* his eyes told her, when the waiter had shown them to their table.

And she liked what Adrian chose, though her stubborn mind insisted on rushing back through the years to her first evening out with Grant, as a pair instead of two in a set. They'd found a small restaurant — not very smart — and knowing that Grant didn't have much money she had purposely missed the starter. In the end, they had settled for fish and chips, sitting cramped at a small table. That meal stayed the nicest Louise had ever had. They had seen themselves as friends, she and Grant; but had they known it, they had already fallen in love.

She jerked her mind from Grant to meet Adrian's smile. He was looking at her gently, eyes sending her a message for which she was as yet unready. It made her wary and put her on her guard. She didn't want to be foolish, to ignore every chance; yet where was the sense in leading him on, unless she were very sure?

But wanting him to know she was enjoying herself, Louise said, quite sincerely: "What a nice place this is! And the food's really out of this world . . ."

"Well, I'd like it to be an evening to remember," Adrian said. "One we can look back upon and treasure. I know I shall never forget it," he whispered. "Nor how beautiful you're looking, tonight . . ."

Louise smiled. Most men said this sort of thing, she'd found — because they really meant it, or felt it was expected of them? It didn't matter: the atmosphere was right for romance, so why should Adrian not respond to its prompting?

"Am I allowed in?" Adrian asked on their return. "It isn't all that late," he pointed out. "I'm sure your friend at Robins Rest needn't even know I've been, if I push the car out, instead of driving it, when I leave."

The stars in his eyes were too bright, now; his glance just a fraction too intimate. She wasn't a prude, Louise told herself, but she had never been any man's easy money, so why make Adrian the exception? "Twenty minutes," she told him. "For coffee — nothing more! If that's okay, then you're very welcome."

"It's not exactly okay . . ." His tone was pleading, even though he endeavoured to laugh. "But I know when I'm beaten," he said, grimacing, "so a coffee it is — and nothing more."

Even so, he tried his luck by letting his kisses grow passionate enough to devour her. Louise, managing to extricate herself as she opened the door for Adrian to leave, felt the sooner he was gone now, the better.

"I can't help it if you do things to me," he protested. "But I've been a good boy, haven't I, Louise? Better than most of them are?"

She sensed jealousy in his voice. Jealousy and hurt: as if he'd hoped, by arousing pity for himself, to end by winning her over. But Louise was adamant. She said, lightly: "If you're like this after a coffee, my lad, then God help the female who gives you drambuie! Now be off with you, Adrian, the granny annexe is definitely closed for the night."

He was back the next evening, arriving unannounced just as Louise was busying herself weeding her strip of garden.

"Hallo . . ." She looked up and smiled at Adrian. "So what brings you here?" she asked.

"You," he said. "Who else?"

He helped her finish the weeding, then followed her indoors, stopping to nibble Louise's ear, having trapped her in the doorway as they entered.

"What other rooms do you have?" Said a little too casually, as soon as they had washed their hands. "I mean, what's through that doorway, for instance?"

Oh, come off it! Louise thought, knowing she frowned. "Which doorway?" she asked, deliberately obtuse.

"The one leading out from the kitchen."

"Nothing that's open to the public," she said.

"I'm not the public . . ." Adrian turned her to face him, his hands spanning her waist. "I'm someone who *loves* you! Yes, I'll risk that word — and I don't use it lightly, my dear."

"It's a word I'd rather you didn't use," she said.

"Not even if I really mean it?"

"I'd still rather you didn't. Let's just be friends . . ."

"No," Adrian said. "No . . ." Again, the hurt in his eyes. "Don't be cold with me, please!" Now, he crushed her against him. "Louise, listen — I can't believe you are really *this* cold."

"You don't know me, that's why . . ." Yet why must she pretend, when she was neither frigid, nor shy? That wasn't her nature, never had been: this was just a facade she had donned. "Ask my parents and any of my friends," she went on, "and they'll all tell you I'm a sworn bachelor girl. Sworn bachelor girls don't talk about loving — not if they're my sort, Adrian."

"I can wait . . . and make you change your mind," he said.

"I don't think so," she told him. "Let's go back to what I said a minute ago — I'd rather we were just friends, okay?"

He moved away to stare from the window to the garden. " 'Just friends' doesn't sound very exciting. Surely, a relationship between a man and a girl should hold a little more than that?" he argued.

"I'm trying to be fair," Louise said.

"It sounds *unfair* to me," he told her. But he let the subject go, saying dully: "All right, fetch out the Scrabble, or a pack of cards — that should sober me up. But you'll have to let me kiss you for a few minutes, first, just to get me in the mood," he said. He stayed late, later than Louise would have wished;

and as his car drew away, she saw it again — a slight figure dodging between the shrubs, then slipping away into the night.

He or she — though Louise was sure it was male — had disappeared, now, but she still felt disturbed and winced against a quick stab of fear. For several minutes, concealed in the shadow of her porch, she stood keeping watch, her breathing painful, heart pounding as she waited. She wouldn't mention this to Eleanor — not yet; but if it happened too often, then she'd have no option; what she had seen was making her nervous. But rather than sit waiting for intruders, she took herself in hand and, back indoors again, was soon undressed and in bed. Nothing happened, as perhaps she had known it wouldn't.

Morning came, and she felt safe once more.

FIVE

She saw a lot of Adrian in the week which followed; though each time, Louise had to be firm or he would probably have stayed until at least three in the morning.

"It's all wrong, you know," he pointed out, when the girl suggested it was getting late. "What do other couples do but stay together as long and as late as they can? Is there some old chaperone tucked away? Some old woman watching your boy friends to see how far they'll go?"

"Well, you're going as far as the gate," Louise told him. "As for your previous remarks," she laughed, "well, let me explain, may I? In the first place we can't be described as a 'couple'. And no, I don't have a chaperone backstage; though had I known I'd meet anyone as dangerous as you, I would certainly have advertised for one, plus a couple of bodyguards, as well. And now, goodnight . . ." She let a kiss touch his lips. "You really must go . . . please, I mean it."

She had been in bed no more than five or six minutes before the telephone started ringing. Tiredness and a reluctance to be disturbed, almost persuaded Louise to ignore it. But finally, she tumbled wearily from the sheets, thinking to herself: If that's Adrian, again, I really *will* be cross!

It wasn't Adrian. Instead, a familiar voice asked: "Louise? This is Grant, I hope you weren't asleep?"

"Not yet . . ." For one almost delirious moment, she found it hard to grasp that this really *was* Grant. Then she realised, brought wide awake by his voice, that he was doing his best to apologise for the horrible silence he'd created at Braintree by announcing Annabel's death.

"The trouble was, I thought you all knew," he said, "and that you were purposely avoiding mentioning Annabel in order not to distress me. I find people do shy away from the subject, and in a way one can't blame them, of course."

"We'd have written and sent flowers, had we known," Louise said. No matter that this wasn't the topic she'd have chosen for her first conversation alone with Grant, it was still good to hear the rich baritone which

60

flowed through his words as he spoke.

"To be truthful, I don't know who wrote and who didn't; I was half out of my mind," he confessed. "I got a friend to answer the letters for me. He made a list, but I couldn't bear to read it."

Louise could understand that. It drove her to say: "Mother felt she'd dropped a clanger, Bernard was embarrassed, and I'm always tongue tied when the wrong thing gets said; but we were all terribly sorry, Grant, and I hope you realised that."

"Bless you, yes I did. I just hoped that I hadn't spoiled you day," he said. "It was great to be with you all, again, and to find the three of you so well."

"And we were pleased to see you."

Grant chuckled. "That doesn't sound like Louise speaking. You're not still embarrassed, are you?"

"Not really . . . To be frank," she had to admit, "I was nearly asleep when the phone rang; so I'm not quite in form, yet, Grant."

Also, she was finding it difficult, she owned, to get back on her old footing with Grant; a lot had happened since she'd broken with him. They hadn't parted as enemies; but everything they'd known, all they had ever loved and shared had inevitably petered out. Stupidly, she found herself longing to say: Do you remember our first meal, together, Grant, in that restaurant somewhere in Chelmsford? You lit the candle in the bottle because you couldn't see me properly, and the waitress frowned when you did it . . .

She heard him say: "So you're living with Eleanor, now? Well, not with her, but beside her in a sort of annexe. Have I got that correct?"

"That's right."

"And is it difficult to find?"

"The annexe, or Robins Rest?"

"Come again, where does Robins Rest fit in?"

"That's the name of Eleanor's house."

"So find one and I'm bound to locate the other? In fact," Grant said, "since I know Millstead and am not all that distance away from you, now, I could easily drive over one evening and would very much like to do so." A pause, then: "May I look in some time? Only if convenient, of course."

"Yes, I'd love that . . ." Why pretend otherwise? Grant's chuckle broke into her thoughts. "I have to ask, in case what's been hinted is true, if you've decided at last to settle down, as they say? With the current boy friend, I mean."

"I'm not with you . . ." Louise felt herself stiffen slightly.

"I seem to have thrown you with that one," he laughed. "However, assuming that things *are* serious, then good for you and I hope you'll be happy — really happy, Louise."

Again, she seemed to stiffen. "Nice of you to say so, but who told you all this, Grant? About this mythical marriage that might take place — should I not have heard of it, myself?"

"Well, you should have heard, yes, if you're booked to be the bride." Grant laughed out loud. "Sorry if I've gaffed; I'm only going by what I was told."

"By whom, for heavens sake?"

"Well, your stepfather told me," he said.

Her own voice was instantly defiant as she answered: "How did he acquire this ridiculous information? He seems to know more than I do about it."

"Search me," Grant said. "Oh, Bernard did remark that you appeared rather reticent on the subject; which was why I made no comment when you and Julia returned. Though Bernard spoke as if it's common news, now."

"It probably is, thanks to Eleanor Russell! I bet she started all this," Louise said. "She and Mother spend hours ringing each other; I think they mostly talk for the sake of talking, never mind the cost of it all. And on that subject," she said, meekly, "I'm not doing *your* phone bill any good, am I? We're not being exactly brief, either."

He said: "Our first conversation for years! As if I'm likely to count the units, Louise . . . So you're not getting married, you say — or are you? It's more than time you settled down, you know."

"That's what they all tell me," she answered.

"Well, they tell me I should re-marry," he said, "but it's not as simple as that. I'm not the sort to jump from marriage to marriage. In any case, I've been shocked — Annabel's death happened all in a matter of hours, Louise; I wasn't even expecting her to die . . ." Grant didn't go into details and she was asking no questions; eleven months couldn't heal a bruised heart, not if you had Grant's nature.

He went on to say: "Now, about my visit, please be candid and don't mind saying if you'd rather I kept away, Louise. I don't want to cause complications. I get a strong feeling that there *is* someone! I can't believe you mean always to stay single."

■ ■ ■ ■

"You could be wrong . . ." Her mind swung
from Grant to Adrian. Between them, they
were making her confused, unsettled, leaving her wondering if, deep down, she *did*
want marriage now. Toes tucked beneath
her long nightie for warmth, she told herself
what she already knew — that Grant had
been her only real love. Now, wanting
desperately to see him, once more, she
found it hard not to sound too eager.

"So which evening, if any, is convenient?"
he asked.

"Friday?" Adrian must stand back for
once. "Are you free that evening, Grant?"

"I'll make it free," he said. "I'll give it
priority; though if for any reason you need
to put me off, I'd better give you my telephone number. You'll notice I'm trying to
be tactful," he laughed. "Believe me, I quite
understand."

But of course, he did not understand,
Louise thought. All the time she was longing to ask him straight over. Come now!
Come tonight! she wanted to say. She bit
her knuckles to hold the words trapped.

"So Friday it is?"

"Yes, any time, however early . . . you'll

find me quite easily," she told him.

"I shall look forward to it," Grant said. "After all this time, how good it will feel to be with you again, Louise . . ."

He surprised himself, saying that; for he learned to think of Louise Mackenzie as a girl he had loved, but would never have; she had made that clear, years back. Yet how often had she come in and out of his thoughts — even into his dreams, Grant recalled. His beautiful Annabel still deserved to be remembered with the love and loyalty she'd inspired; he could even have felt guilty, Grant owned, if he thought too much of Louise.

After he had rung off the room seemed empty, as if she'd lost Grant a second time, Louise thought: all excitement seemed hushed to sadness. She didn't thank Bernard for talking about her, nor Eleanor for starting a silly rumour; but there it was, people did gossip in this world, mostly not meaning to be unkind, nor realising what might result. And perhaps, after all, they were not to be blamed for viewing Adrian's arrival with hope; what frightened Louise was that he, in his turn, might share the self-same ideas.

Lost in thought, she felt restless and unsettled, now. Having linked up with Grant once more, she was certain she would never want anyone else — not Adrian, nor any man. Grant's reappearance into her life had seemed to cause an emotional upheaval; she even wondered, slipping back into bed, how she had endured those last four years and the accompaying loneliness they'd brought.

But in it all, she had to be fair to Adrian, not to use him as a comforter, a stop-gap. Surely it was kinder to make it clear that what he chased was nothing but a shadow?

Six

She got up early; and there was Kim feeding the birds — sparrows and blackbird, their own tame robin, while the starlings and gulls were still away on their respective sleeping grounds.

Louise waved to Kim, prepared her own breakfast, which she ate out of doors seated on the steps in the first of the day's sunshine. She was tired, but speaking to Grant overnight had been worth losing sleep for, she told herself, though she wondered if she were being a fool in allowing him to visit the annexe.

Yet Grant was a friend, more than a friend, and she couldn't resist letting him come now that he'd suggested it. She would accept he was a man still grieving for his wife, and she must not let him know how much he still meant. When Grant came, it would be as Annabel's widower, not as Louise's lover.

Eleanor had a coffee morning, that day. Louise offered to help; but Eleanor, as always, had her own group of helpers already on duty. She was busy, but found time to talk to Louise.

"Your mother phoned," she said. "She's invited me for a long weekend at Braintree, dear. So I think I'll go fairly soon. A nice break, don't you think?"

Louise nodded. "Yes, a good idea . . ." She helped herself to a biscuit and smiled at Eleanor who was enjoying herself no end. "Mother's always pleased to see you," she agreed.

She tried to summon up the courage to ask Eleanor to be a little more discreet in what she said to the Driscolls. But there were no words to say what Louise had in mind; and in any case, halfway through a coffee morning was no time for discussion. In the end, she let it go. In time, when these rumours came to nothing, people would soon lose interest.

She saw Adrian that evening and the one which followed. He had somehow acquired a poisoned finger; for very little, he'd have been bad tempered.

"I'm sorry if I sound a misery," he said, "but the throbbing and the pain's driving me crazy. It's really giving me hell . . ."

Louise looked at his finger and felt sorry for Adrian. On his way home from the office he had seen his doctor; but it was no use thinking of lancing for quite a few days, he'd been told.

"By then, I'll be up the wall," he declared. "God knows how I'll stick it much longer."

Letting his head rest on her shoulder, as a child might nestle against its mother, Louise wished he need not be unwell. She wished it for his own sake; and also because cosseting and tending him as she must, could only add to Adrian's belief that she cared for him more than she'd say. Yet could he have known it, her true concern was out of the annexe to wherever it was Grant might be at this moment. Was she letting this man take over, again, as he had in those never to be forgotten days when they had come within an ace of marriage? She had hoped, when other men entered her life, that she might have overcome her love for Grant, but it had not worked out that way. Even now, much as she liked Adrian and much as she felt concerned for him that day, her mind stayed on Grant.

"Kiss me," Adrian said. He had snuggled closer; and now she wished she need not feel so apprehensive, so afraid of finding herself involved with someone she could not love. And it made things even harder that, as he knew her better, Adrian would become more demanding, more possessive, not wanting to take things step at a time, but to plunge straight from A to Z. Quite natural, yes, Louise told herself; but how would he react when the time came to say that she wanted to call a halt?

Adrian stirred. "I *do* love you, Louise. If only we could always be together . . ."

Time, now, to call that halt? Louise wasn't sure; but she answered, knowing this had to be said: "Don't get too fond of me, Adrian."

Eyes hurt and accusing, he asked, tightly: "Did you *have* to say that? Especially tonight . . . at this moment?"

"It has to be said at some time," she told him. "I'm sorry, but it does, Adrian."

"Because we haven't known each other long, it that it? God, it doesn't take months to fall in love. Sometimes, it can happen all in seconds."

She tried to keep her voice gentle. "Do you *really* love me?"

"Yes, I do . . . and you know I do. People say, how can you tell when it's love? Well, you know from the moment it happens." Adrian stared beyond her, speaking moodily, now. "When did I first know? The day I met you!"

"Well, let's not talk about it, now . . ." She heard her voice grow soothing, aware she felt mean staving him off, but seeing no other alternative. "You've got this wretched bad finger," she pointed out. "Why not sit back and take things quietly?"

Panic or temper — she couldn't tell which — made his voice suddenly furious. "For God's sake, Louise, you're not tired of me, are you? *Why* mayn't I say that I love you? You're always putting the brake on, fencing me off. What the hell's gone wrong between us? Look, you've got to understand," he sounded desperate, now, "what a lot you mean to me, my darling . . ."

She had him quietened, at last; persuaded him to rest until he was fit enough to drive. He'd keep away until his finger had been lanced, he promised. Then they'd make a fresh start and sort things out . . . talk about it quietly and calmly.

SEVEN

Grant had just pulled up behind a line of traffic at the top of Angel Hill in Bury St Edmunds, when he heard an urgent tapping on the passenger window, causing him to jerk round and stare.

He had supposed it was someone to do with his practice. Instead, to his surprise, there was Marian Taylor. Marian, who over the last few years had seldom, if ever, crossed Grant's mind.

The traffic ahead was threatening to move. Grant wound the window down and Marian chirped: "Well, fancy seeing you, of all people! Grant, what a lovely surprise!" He might have left it at a smile, calling: "Oh, hallo!" But now she was asking: "Any chance of a lift? And may I get in before somebody runs me over?"

He could hardly leave her stranded; and so all within seconds, she was there in his car, right beside him. Grant gulped. He was not pleased to see this girl; but good manners demanded that he asked, kindly: "How are you, after all this time?"

"I'm fine," she answered. "And you, Grant?"

"I'm fine, too," he told her.

"And working here in Bury, so a little bird told me . . ."

"That's right." A poor conversation, this.

"I work here, too," Marian said.

They'd reached the edge of the town. "Not quite the place to park," Grant remarked with the grin she had once adored. "So, quite briefly, it's nice to see you, again; and if you're going my way, perhaps I can give you a lift?"

Marian said: "Well, I always bring my car, Grant, but today it's gone in to be serviced. If you're bound for any place near Linsell Green, I'd be terribly grateful."

"I could actually go that way," Grant obliged. "That's where you live, then?" he asked.

"Yep — for several weeks, now . . ." She wouldn't bore him with details; she was too busy noticing that Grant was driving an almost brand new Jag. He was doing very nicely, then, she thought.

"You're married now, of course?" he asked, smiling.

"Not yet . . ." She showed him her ring-less hand. "Still waiting for the right guy," she told him.

"Like that?" His own laugh was faintly embarrassed, and Marian put in: "Grant, I have to say this — I was terribly sorry to hear the sad news. Eleven months ago, wasn't it?"

"Twelve months, now. . . ." He wished he hadn't mentioned the date. It had dawned upon him, a few hours earlier, that this was the first anniversary; it sickened him to think about it.

The year had seemed endless. He had spent his days thinking: 'This time last year, we did such-and-such a thing. Annabel was alive and we were both happy, never dreaming what was to happen . . .' He had willed the hours to pass, held memories at arm's length, never knowing what nightmares he'd dream. He knew Annabel would have hated him to grieve as he had; and now he wanted, for her sake as well as his own, to endeavour to enjoy life, again. She would not have been hurt, could even have been pleased, to know he had turned to Louise for comfort; Grant had never known Annabel to be jealous.

Marian was still commiserating with him. "I didn't know," she was saying, "until

Eleanor told me. And *she* didn't know until after Louise had been to see Julia and Bernard."

"That's right . . ." Grant nodded. "I saw Louise at Braintree, when I looked in on the Driscolls. Someone else who's still single — Louise, I mean." He let a chuckle run into his voice as he asked: "What's the matter with all these East Anglian men that they're letting pretty girls like yourself and Louise slip through the net, huh?"

"Oh, but Louise *is* going to marry," she said.

"Really?" She saw his eyebrows shoot up. "I thought that was just a rumour."

"Rumour, my foot!" Marian scoffed. "You can take it from me that's no rumour . . ." Well, Eleanor Russell had good as said Louise was nicely fixed up, now; so it wasn't exactly a lie, was it? And why should she worry, if it were? Louise had already had her chance. If Grant was back in the market, Marian would pull out all the stops to get him. She had tried once and failed; but she was wiser, now . . .

Grant said: "Well, according to Bernard Driscoll, there *is* someone in the offing; but when I mentioned it to Louise, she was absolutely definite that she isn't getting married and isn't even engaged. So who's right and who's wrong?" he asked.

Marian shrugged. She could not read Grant's thoughts, only knew that she had never ceased to love this man — and that now she would do anything, however underhand, in order to win his affection. Yes, this time she *would* be the winner. And since all was fair in love and war, what was wrong with garnishing things a little? Anything to put Grant off. She could always say, if he caught her out, that she had only repeated what someone had said.

Grant's frown and his completely bewildered expression prompted her to say: "Well, I know it *is* true; and from what I've heard, the wedding has to be soon. I'm not a gossip," she told him, "I hate that sort of thing; but I have to tell you, Grant, in case you should write and perhaps congratulate Louise."

One doesn't congratulate the *girl!* he almost said; but instead, asked, his voice sharp: "Tell me what? I don't get your meaning."

Marian grimaced. Having got this far, she just had to sound convincing, she told herself. She loathed Louise Mackenzie, anyway.

"Well, this is in confidence," she said, slowly, "so for God's sake don't say *I* told you. It's what is classically called a shotgun wedding; and I'd imagine Louise is keeping quiet because she isn't very proud of the fact."

She was amazed how plausible her voice sounded; even more amazed that all these lies should tumble out as easily and naturally as if they had been the truth. She knew Louise wasn't pregnant, but she wasn't having Grant cast his eyes in that direction. So let him think a baby was on the way; and Grant; who liked his friends to conform to convention, would definitely not go near.

And, yes, he was shocked. It was written on his face; despite his clenched jaw, Grant couldn't conceal his reaction. Anyone but Louise! was all he could think, asking: "Are you sure about this?" — knowing he'd begun to feel queasy. He had never been a prude and God knew he was accustomed to this sort of thing, and worse, in the course of his daily professional life; but always connected with people who were strangers — not someone like Louise, whom he'd loved.

Marian saw his change of colour and felt smugly triumphant. "Well, don't let it worry you." She patted his knee. "I've only told you because, as I've said, Louise is rather touchy on the subject, which is quite understandable, I guess."

Grant said nothing, just wished Marian out of his car, relieved when she said: "Well, slow down, now, because here's my little bungalow — the one on the corner, Grant. Thanks a million for the lift. I'm sorry I had to be blunt about Louise, but —" She let the subject go with a shake of her head. "However, to speak of something else — won't you come in, now you're here?"

"No, I really do have another engagement."

"No time even for a cuppa?" Marian let disappointment shadow her face. "It's just about ages since we last met," she said, "we must have bookfuls of news to exchange." She added, making no move as yet: "Let me be frank on one point, Grant. I know how you're placed. It's early days, yet; so I certainly wouldn't take advantage — if you get me? Not for your sake, or for Annabel's," she told him.

"No, of course not . . ." Grant was embarrassed, now. More so, when Marian drew out a pad on which she scribbled her telephone number. Having handed this to him, she said, with meaning: "Any evening you happen to feel lonely, or depressed! Ring first, in case I'm out; if I'm home, then I'll love to see you, okay?"

To his surprise, she left a light perfumed

kiss on his cheek. "You poor devil . . ." Her voice was thick. "Let me help you if I can, won't you?"

Grant waited until she had entered her gate, then swung his car round to get back on the road which would take him the five miles to Millstead. He had no intention of calling upon Marian; certainly not to spend an evening with her. Had he wanted this girl when Louise turned him down, he could easily have asked her instead of Annabel. The truth was, Marian hadn't appealed . . . and still didn't appeal.

But recalling what she'd said about Louise, he felt upset to a point of sickness. He had loved Louise even more than he had grown to love Annabel; but she had point-blank refused to have him. She had been bitter and cynical on the subject of marriage; and nothing, Grant had found, could shift her from the notion that more were doomed for failure, than weren't.

But time changed people and he'd been relieved that a lot of her bitterness had softened. Even Bernard's hint that Louise had someone else, hadn't deterred Grant from promising himself that he might even yet win Louise. Something very precious had passed between them, and Grant knew it had never quite died.

But, hearing that Louise was carrying a child, he knew it was her lover, Grant's unknown rival, who held the prior claim. A state of affairs he had not expected, it made him feel sad and ill.

But he would see Louise that evening, having promised to call; and naturally, he would not repeat one word of what Marian had just said. Only hoped that being alone with Louise would not stir too many memories within him, making him long for her, again.

It had been hard enough living through Annabel's death: having to pick up the threads, once more, and to face the fact that she was gone. He'd surmounted one fearful obstacle in his life; but to have a second struggle with his heart and emotions seemed more than Grant could face. Yes, he'd see Louise this once, then would call it a day and keep right away from this girl.

The footsteps on the drive leading to the annexe were too familiar to be Grant Sullivan's, even though it was Grant she was expecting. Perplexed, Louise went to the door.

And there stood Adrian. "Just a quickie," he said. "I'm off to the surgery about my finger. I can't take any more, Louise."

"It looks frightful," she sympathised.

Adrian nodded. "I'm due there in less than half an hour, but I had to see you first — just to kiss you and say I love you . . ."

She felt ashamed it was disappointment she felt. No, not exactly disappointment: it was hard to say just how she *did* feel, just then. For she was fond of Adrian, and though she could not love him she did not want him hurt, either.

"Until tomorrow," he whispered against her hair. "I'll be okay, once this finger's put right. And if I'm not —" Despite his pain, he gave a small wicked laugh. "— I'll have to come here and go to bed . . . yes?"

She couldn't think of a smart reply to that; and in any case, he'd already glanced at his watch. "Hell, I'll be late!" he muttered. One long drawn-out kiss, followed by a second, and Adrian had left, turning to wave before getting into his car. Returning to the annexe, Louise felt bothered. She could not continue to let him come if he really felt as loving as he said; it was neither fair nor kind. Yet how did she break this alliance up? She had once hurt Grant and could still feel guilty.

She would hate to do the same to Adrian.

Not that she need have any cause for guilt, Louise consoled herself. If he had straightway fallen for her, it was not through any encouragement given; things had just worked out that way. He would be angry and jealous if he knew another man would be calling upon her that same evening; except that Grant wasn't just 'another man'. Their old relationship was over, but they were still friends in a way no one else would understand.

Impatient to see him, Louise could not remember if Grant had named a specific time, or had simply said he would call. And so, ears strained, she listened for his car. Listened and listened, feeling every minute wasted until she could know he had come.

EIGHT

And then, joy, there he was! Grant, striding along the drive, making straight for her little home. She was glad that, for once, Robins Rest was empty, Eleanor having taken Kim to a concert as part of the girl's birthday present.

"I'll give her a little something to spend when the actual day comes," Eleanor said, "but really Kim's life is too restricted! She must occasionally go out and enjoy herself, instead of sticking here, all the time."

"You would think she'd go out with Brock," Louise said.

Eleanor let out a snort. "He's nobody's catch," she said, "he's a right slacker, is Brock. Anyway, I'm taking Kim to this concert and we might have a bite at a restaurant, after, which means we'll be fairly late home. But you'll be all right, Louise?"

So off these two had gone and in consequence there were no prying eyes to note

Grant's arrival and to pass on the news to Julia. Louise ran to the door to let him in.

"You found it, then?" she said.

Grant's smile was polite. "No problem at all," he told her.

"Well, do come in . . ." She felt suddenly shy; and Grant wasn't helping by appearing ill at ease, as if he felt he'd no right to be there. She had expected the man she had known four years back — even the Grant who had phoned her, that week — but this man was almost a stranger.

Impulsively, she asked: "Have I put you in a spot? I mean, was there something else you'd planned to do?" Might as well be frank with him, she told herself, thinking: Oh, Grant, please be nice! I've looked forward to this, so much . . .

"No, I'd nothing else planned." He glanced around as he spoke. "This is very pleasant, Louise . . . the first granny annexe I've ever seen." His voice was kind and he, himself, was being kind; but this still wasn't the Grant she had known, he had never been pedantic, as now. He looked thoroughly upset, Louise decided.

"If I make coffee, will you have some?" she asked. "Or a drink? Or both? And will you risk a sponge I've made?"

He grinned and just for one brief moment

it was the smile she had always known. "I'll risk the sponge and settle for a coffee," he said. "I do remember you were always a very good cook and your coffee would do justice to an expert." Seeing to these things, waiting upon Grant, made Louise feel as if she sparkled all over: almost like being married to him, she thought — as if she'd suddenly found herself his bride.

And Grant, who could always say the right thing, was ready to praise Louise's sponge and the little biscuits she had made. Was ready, after these had been consumed, to go with her into her little workroom where he looked at some of her portraits. The half finished portrait of Adrian's Fritz had been pushed into the background for that evening.

Grant was more impressed by her work than she'd expected, saying: "You're really clever at this! — just the right touch, Louise. We all knew you could paint — but not to do this sort of thing and to make a living from it."

"Well, it's not original — the idea, I mean," Louise was bound to admit, "but it's certainly cottoned on. I often wish I could paint people," she confessed. "Animals seem easier. I enjoy painting them, anyway."

"You're very talented," Grant said. *But not loveable, or desirable!* Louise thought, feeling sad. Grant hadn't even kissed her when he entered. It wasn't that she wanted him to fall upon his knees: she'd have hated him to say it ought to have been she, and not Annabel, he married. No, nothing like that, Louise told herself; but at least he could pretend to be pleased to see her.

Yet she couldn't have said Grant was at all unfriendly. In some strange, sad way he was trying to be nice while determinedly keeping his distance. But why? Louise wondered. He should know her well enough to feel perfectly at home and safe in her presence. But the way he was behaving, she could only assume Grant was writing FINISH to it all.

She would have liked to show him her other rooms: an intimacy she'd refrained from where Adrian was concerned, since he would only have seen it as an invitation leading them both to her bedroom. But Grant was different; he would appreciate that naturally she'd be proud of her little home and would have nothing else in mind.

Yet as he was, now, Louise doubted he'd have shown even the smallest interest, except to say it was very nice. But he did volunteer that he, himself, had a flat.

"Rented," he explained. "You know those service affairs with a restaurant attached?" He also told her about his work. He had settled in well, liked his partners, and had plenty on hand.

Suddenly, he half rose in his chair; and she knew he was fumbling for a tactful excuse whereby he could escape from the annexe. She helped him out by saying: "I'm keeping you, Grant. I mustn't do that — and in any case," she fibbed, "I've a portrait to finish, this evening."

"Well . . ." He stood up, now, and let his eyes meet her own. "You would like the truth, wouldn't you, Louise? I shouldn't have come, should I?"

"Why not?" Shocked by his statement, she asked: "What have I done, or said?"

"Nothing that could give offence," Grant assured her, "and I haven't been bored, in any way. You've stayed the same sweet girl you've always been and I've loved seeing you, again." A nerve in his jaw had started to tick; he was either upset, embarrassed, or both, but his voice stayed level and calm. "I'll be frank, I came earlier, a little before six — before I was expected, I suppose. Anyway, I had to clear off, again, because you and the boy friend were saying good-bye. I could hardly interrupt, could I?" he asked. "I think we would all have been embarrassed."

Louise could only stare, and Grant went on, still in the same calm voice: "So I went for a drive, to give you time to cool off. Things being as they are, you can't blame me, Louise, if I feel an intruder here, tonight. And that's a role I'm not accustomed to playing."

A quick burst of temper made her exclaim: "You shouldn't have come back, feeling like that. I don't ask anyone to visit me on sufferance."

"Not on sufferance," Grant said, "the truth is, I've come back too late, Louise. Just as before, I was much too soon. I can't win, can I? But never mind — as I say, it's been great seeing you. . . ."

As he walked down the drive, Grant felt he'd be glad to be home again. His encounter with Marian had upset him enough; but then to see Louise in another man's embrace seemed, somehow, the last straw. Well, he knew now that he had a rival . . . and unhappily, in view of what Marian had said, he couldn't and mustn't compete. He could only walk out and stay away from Louise — lose himself in hard work as he'd learned to do, and turn his back upon self pity.

NINE

Almost as Louise finished breakfast, next day, Adrian rang to say he was still having trouble. Once again, they had put off lancing his finger.

"Talk about a messed-up weekend," he groused. "I can't drive and I'm company for no one, as I am, so this means I shall have to wait until Monday before I can see you, again."

"Never mind . . ." It was just a little disconcerting that she had to experience relief; but she was still smarting badly over Grant's visit and did not want company, that day. She'd had a bad night after Grant had gone, small wonder she felt washed out and tired.

"Well, I've plenty of work to do," she said, "so perhaps, as far as I'm concerned, it's as well I shall be tied to the house." She had been agreeably surprised by further replies in response to her most recent advert; these, at least, could console her, she thought.

Adrian said: "Well, don't sound so damn glad to be working! I'm fed up! Last night I hardly saw you. Five minutes — that was all! I only just had time to kiss you . . ."

Could he not have left that last sentence unsaid? Louise felt herself wince. For the kisses he had given had all been observed and she was horribly afraid Grant might even have thought she had purposely staged that little scene.

Her face grew hot at the suggestion. She would hate him to think that of her.

"Louise — are you there?" Adrian enquired.

"Yes, I'm still here," she told him. "Would aspirin help, do you think?"

"Nothing and no one helps — only you! I'm bloody fed up," Adrian said. "Sorry — I've got an attack of the blues." A kiss came her way, followed by another. "All my love until Monday."

Louise replaced the phone and moved to the window. Outside, a light rain pattered down moistening the lawn and encouraging the flowers to freshen under its coolness. She wished Adrian could have been coming, that day — an outing was just what she wanted. Apart from pleasure gained, it might also have helped to ease the bitter hurt Grant's visit had left; though that, she supposed, was a poor reason for wanting Adrian's company.

And then the phone rang, again. This time it was Grant. "I need to apologise, Louise," he said. "You very kindly invited me to your little home, put yourself out to be the perfect hostess — and in return, I behaved badly. You must have been glad when I left . . ."

"That's all right." She ought to be cool, even cold; but somehow that wasn't possible with Grant; they were too close to stay enemies.

"Well, I'm sorry," he told her. "I hope I'm forgiven, though I don't deserve to be. I realise your life is your own affair. You're free, grown up and of sane mind; whatever you do is absolutely none of my business."

Which means you no longer care, either way! she thought, feeling hurt. His phrase, 'it's absolutely none of my business' was proof that their own break was final.

She let a few seconds pass to regain her breath, then said: "That's okay, no apology needed; I was still pleased to see you," she told him. Tempted to add that she was sorry she'd embarrassed him, she knew she couldn't talk about Adrian Pryce as if she'd cause to feel ashamed of his friendship. In any case, Grant had already made it clear that he wasn't likely to call in future.

"Just so long as you aren't upset," he said. She could feel him preparing to hang up and disappointment knocked her off balance. "Let's leave it at that, shall we?" he suggested. "Take care of yourself and be happy, always, won't you?"

When the phone had replaced, she sat staring at it, as if willing it to start ringing again, bringing Grant's voice back into her home and, with it, something of himself. Well, of course he would not wish to further their acquaintance, let alone resurrect what was over.

But she did wish that Grant needn't be quite so sure that she and Adrian were hooked on each other. He'd be sending teaspoons or a toast rack, soon, Louise thought, turning her back on the phone, angry with the tears now falling. Could he only know where her true preference lay . . . But he didn't, and that was just as well, or he really *would* be embarrassed.

She saw Adrian several times during the week which followed. They spent their Saturday on the coast, mostly at Southwold, the sea fresh as a newly run bath. It was cool, but they braved the water for a swim; towelled each other dry, then walked till they were warm; and if Louise did occasionally call to mind two blue-grey eyes and a fascinating smile, she still wouldn't let that spoil her day, or allow any hint of comparison.

To Adrian's annoyance, they needed to return a full hour earlier than he'd hoped. Louise had a client coming to see her — and clients had priority, she told him.

"Male or female?" Jealousy ran into his voice.

"Female, for what it matters."

"She couldn't have made it last night, by any chance?"

"She asked for tonight," Louise said.

"You should have told her you were already booked up." Adrian could even have been angry, now. "Saturday is *our* day," he said. "She wanted telling that you're not at her beck and call, and that sometimes you've other things to do."

"Say that too many times and there'd be no clients!" But Louise let Adrian hold her against his heart, allowed one last lingering kiss.

"I'll be phoning," he said. "Keep next week free. You will, won't you?" he coaxed.

She watched his car draw away and wished, as he left, that she could feel a little less unsettled. After all, it had been a happy day and she had loved being by the sea. Back at the annexe, she found a note for Eleanor caught in the flap of her letter box — a message from the local bridge club. She was just going to deliver the note to Eleanor, when her client rang to say she had a migraine and dared not drive, that evening. Could she ask for Monday, instead?

Adrian should be there to hear this! Louise thought, suppressing a chuckle as she answered. But business was business, so what did it matter if appointments did have to be switched around? It wasn't a life and death matter. Having coped with the lady, she went to the house where Eleanor let her in. Marian was there, seated in the lounge, cigarette in one hand, a smile on her face.

Or was it a smirk? Louise wondered.

She said, "Hallo," and tried to let her own smile encourage a little friendship. It was ridiculous of Marian to bear malice this way, but nothing would change now. She let the thought slip away while Eleanor complained what nit-wits some people were. "Fancy putting that note through Louise's door, when it plainly says Robins Rest!" she said. "Half the world can't read, that's the trouble. However, join us for a drink, dear," she invited.

"Thanks, I will . . ." Not that Louise

wanted to be there while Marian remained, but one couldn't be unsociable, she reflected. "Just as well I came in when I did," she remarked. "I had a telephone call from a client, almost as I opened the door."

"Louise is doing very well with her portraits," Eleanor said, speaking proudly, as if this were her own daughter. "I wish I could paint half as well."

"I'd hate it." Marian never minced her words. "Cooped up painting cats and dogs for old women with too much money to spend!"

"Men come as well," Louise told her.

"Sure, we've just seen one bring you home." Marian laughed, and Eleanor said: "We'll get round to that in a minute, dear. Let's all have a drink, first. Here's yours . . ." She handed a full glass to Marian. "And now *you* tell us," she said, addressing Louise, "if that handsome young fellow who keeps calling upon you is 'just one of those things', to quote yourself, or really serious, this time?"

"Just one of those things," Louise answered.

"Well, he's frightfully good looking," Eleanor said. "Marian and I had a good stare! You can certainly pick them, can't you?"

A laugh, and Louise hoped the subject was dismissed, except that Marian was still smirking. No doubt she was inwardly crowing to herself because it wasn't Grant, Louise decided. Talk about jealousy and strife! Not that she would let this girl upset her; once she'd left, she'd forget her, completely.

Refusing to be baited, she turned away; though had Eleanor not been talking, claiming attention, she might well have paused if only for seconds, to wonder just what Marian *did* have in mind to give her face such a cunning expression. But she resolutely refused to look at her, and Marian, who'd begun to feel slightly bored, soon rose and said she must go.

The door closed upon her, Eleanor said: "You look tired, Louise. Are you?"

"A little, yes . . ." For she had had a long day, and those walks by the sea, the strong salt air, and now this exhausting half hour with Marian, had made her feel tipsy with fatigue.

She went back to the annexe and once indoors, tried to forget Marian. Too bad she had come into their midst; but no one could stop the incautious Eleanor from making all people welcome.

97

TEN

And then Monday, Kim Logan's twentieth birthday. "A lovely age to be!" Eleanor enthused. She had given the girl a nice money present; and Louise, on a less grand scale, did the same. "Though she'll spend it right away," was Eleanor's prediction.

"I had three birthday cards, Miss Mackenzie," Kim reported. "Yours, Mrs Russell's, and one from me friend what's maid up at the vicarage. It's nice to be remembered," she said. Left at that, the birthday would have satisfied Kim; but when Eleanor gave her the afternoon off, she could not get the dishes washed quickly enough before dashing upstairs for her coat.

"I'm going to Bury St Edmunds," she announced. "I might do some shopping there."

Ungainly though she was, Kim felt almost regal as she made her way to the village. The service bus wasn't due, Kim knew that, but awaiting its arrival was part of the outing.

Marian came by, driving her Fiat which she promptly screeched to a halt.

"Hall-o! Who's doing the housework, then?" she wanted to know, beaming at the girl. "You look set for a real binge, are you?"

"Well, it's me birthday," Kim explained. "Mrs Russell and Miss Mackenzie have given me some money, so I'm off to do some shopping."

"Well, you can wait till Kingdom come for that bus," Marian said. "I'm not working today, so I'll give you a lift both ways, if you like. That's assuming you're going to Bury St Edmunds — okay?"

"Oh, nice . . ." Kim was soon settled in the Fiat. "Though I don't really like troubling you, Miss."

"No trouble!" Marian started the car. She had already decided why she'd give this girl a lift: she had something in mind and Kim seemed the ideal person. She was simple, yes, but so much the better: simple folk were often more easily managed and did not as a rule ask questions. "On our way back," she said, her voice casual, "there's something I'd like you to do, if you will. It's only a small matter."

"So long as it don't make me late," the

girl bargained, "I wouldn't like to let Mrs Russell down — not after her being kind enough to give me the afternoon off, Miss Taylor. I said I'd be back by teatime."

Marian laughed. "Good grief!" she exclaimed. "I only want you to deliver a letter! That's not asking much, is it?"

"Have you got it with you, then?" Kim enquired.

"No, that's the whole point," Marian said. "I don't want it posted in a pillar box, but I'll explain all that later." A fast driver, she reached Bury St Edmunds even sooner than Kim had expected. "Well, here we are!" Marian said. "Now listen, I'll park here on Angel Hill and leave you to do your shopping, shall I? Take your time. You'll find me here when you come back — unless you'd like me to go with you?"

Kim didn't like. If she does that, she thought, she's bound to say not to be extravagant, or to buy something plain and useful. But her eyes lit up when Marian said: "Look, *I* haven't given you a present, yet! And if you're going to deliver that letter for me, you'll deserve a little extra, won't you? How's that?" She put some money into Kim's lap.

"Oh, Miss Taylor!" The girl was covered with confusion. "You didn't ought to give me all this," she protested. "It's only me birthday, you know . . ." But she took it, though she still felt Marian had been too generous — this was more than Mrs Russell had given her.

"Well, don't keep thanking me," Marian said. "Just trot along and have some fun, okay?" She watched the girl making towards the shops: bought a parking ticket, then settled down to amuse herself with a crossword.

Minutes later, her restless mind queried: I wonder if I dare phone Grant, later? She had done so twice since he had given her that lift, and each time he'd sounded off-hand. Marian pulled a face. "What's the matter with the man?" she muttered to herself, irritated now. "He can't *still* be grieving for someone he married out of pique?" And he couldn't have seen Louise, she decided, or Eleanor would for sure have found out and passed the news around.

So what did this mean? Marian wondered. That Grant had already found a woman? Well, she wouldn't give up — not she! Sooner or later, she'd catch Grant off guard . . . when he'd be very glad to take what she'd offer.

Kim took Marian at her word and was gone some time, returning well laden and looking pleased, having spent all but 50p.

"I got some undies, a blouse and a neck-lace, Miss Taylor. And I bought meself a cardigan and a handbag," she said. "Like to see what I got?"

Marian squinted into the various bags, thinking: God, what a load of trash! "I also got some tights," Kim continued, having raked among her purchases some more.

"You did pretty well, then," Marian allowed, starting the car as she spoke. She drove on awhile, then: "Now for that job you promised you'd do, remember?" Kim nodded. She was still sorting through what she'd bought and Marian felt impatient.

Having reached the place she wanted, she stopped the car, turning to the girl, sternly. "Now pay heed to what I'm saying, Kim," she said, "because this is very important. So please give me your full attention."

"Yes, Miss." Like being back at school, Kim thought.

"Okay, then," Marian said. "Now you see that yellow door, over there? Well, this envelope is to be pushed through the letter box — couldn't be simpler, could it? Don't knock, or ring the bell, and don't hang about. Come straight back to me, as soon as you've done the job."

Kim looked at the envelope Marian had

given her. "What a funny way it's been addressed," she said. "It's like each letter's been cut out from a newspaper or magazine. Who stuck them on, Miss Taylor?"

Marian let out a gasp of impatience. "For God's sake, *must* you hold an inquest, Kim? I thought I'd made it worth your while to do this little job! Be sensible and do as you're asked. I'll pull round the corner, because I shouldn't be parked just here."

A little reluctantly, Kim got out; did as instructed and took good care to be as quick as she could. There was something about this she didn't much like, but Miss Taylor had given her a lot of money as well as a lift both ways in her car, so maybe she shouldn't ask questions.

And indeed, Marian was fully intending to make quite sure Kim *didn't* ask questions; more than that, she meant to see she kept quiet. Half a mile along the road, she drew the car to a halt.

Kim turned her marmalade eyes upon Marian and waited, half afraid. "No, there's nothing to be scared of," she was told. "But the point is, no one is to know about this, and you are *not* to ask questions, get me? No one's to be told! Not even Mrs Russell, or Louise."

Kim nodded. "Yes, all right." She sounded

nervous.

"I hope you mean that." Marian started the car, her laugh artificial as she told her: "Well, between ourselves, it's just a bit of fun I'm having with someone, Kim. But they must never know who sent that letter, or the whole joke will be ruined . . ." She felt certain she could trust this simple girl; but even so, would not let her leave the car until she had repeatedly given her word that she would not tell a soul.

"I know you won't, if you say not." She patted Kim's hand.

"Yes, you're right, I never splits if I promise! And thank you for me present, Miss Taylor . . ."

Eleanor was over at the granny annexe, and saying that she couldn't imagine who would have the place when Louise married and left.

"I'd hate it to lie empty," she said, already sad.

"But who said I was likely to marry?" Louise asked.

"Oh, my dear, of course you will! I mean, look at you, pretty as a picture and you know it! Besides, what about that gorgeous dark haired young man I'm still hoping to meet? Even if he does get sent on his way, the same as too many already have, surely Grant will be lucky, this time?"

"Why Grant?" She had to hold her breath as she said it.

"Now, Louise, what an empty question! What man of his age would stay a widower for long? Besides, we all know he cared for you, dear . . ."

"You read too many novels and think too much about romance!" Louise laughed, giving Eleanor a hug. "I wonder how Kim's getting on?" She did not want to speak about either man. But there was one matter she felt should be discussed; should have been mentioned days back, in fact. She brought it out into the open now, saying: "Eleanor, have you ever thought you'd seen Brock in the garden, fairly late in the evening? At first, I decided he was waiting for Kim, but I think she was already in bed."

"Brock wouldn't be waiting for Kim, I'm quite sure. Nor would any of the village lads," Eleanor said. "She doesn't have a young man. Besides Kim is always early to bed." A rather sharp glance came Louise's way. "Did you not call to whoever this was and ask what they were doing?"

"No, I didn't, though I should have done, of course. As I say, I thought someone might be waiting for Kim — at least, I hoped they were." Louise bit her lip. "I didn't know what to do; and almost at once, they disappeared into the road."

"Only once, I take it?"

"No, twice," Louise admitted. "I should have mentioned this before."

Eleanor pursed her lips. "If you think you see anyone again, however late, then give me a tinkle and we'll both go out. I'll take my walking stick with me."

Louise was just going to say she didn't fancy being coshed, when Kim's stocky figure turned into the drive, the several bags she carried proving Eleanor to be right — she must have spent every penny, they decided.

Eleanor steered both girls towards the house. "I've a cake for you, Kim," she said, smiling. "In fact, a small celebration tea, because one doesn't have a birthday every day!"

"Thank you, Mrs Russell . . ." But Kim looked uneasy. Even after she had put all she'd bought on display, she still appeared nervous, Louise thought. As if something had happened to trouble her.

"Well, you certainly bought plenty," Eleanor observed, "and a very pretty cardigan you've got there, Kim. Very pretty, indeed."

"I'm afraid I spent rather a lot," Kim

confessed. "I'm rather low in drawers and things, so I thought I'd set myself up."

"I wish she'd call them pants, or knickers," Eleanor said, when Kim had gone. "The word *drawers* always sounds rude, somehow — well, vulgar, anyway." A pause, then, a dubious note in her voice: "She bought rather a lot with our money, didn't she? I'm not suggesting she's been shoplifting, Louise; she's as honest as honest, is Kim. But —" Eleanor frowned, worried now, "except for what we gave her, she only had two pounds."

"Unless she had more money than you thought?" Louise suggested. "Or she might have drawn some out from savings?"

"Well, maybe you're right . . ." Eleanor still looked doubtful.

Kim was also worried. *Whatever have I done?* she kept asking herself. *I'm sure something ain't* right . . . The money Marian had given seemed an awful lot for doing nothing more than stuff an envelope through a door; Kim didn't like the feel of it, at all. "I didn't ought to have done it," she whispered to herself. "Not without asking what the letter was about: it looked a funny sort of envelope to me . . ." And the trouble was, having spent the money which Marian had given in the form of a bribe,

Kim felt in a cleft stick. A pity she had met Miss Taylor, she thought, though the cash had been more than welcome. And at least she had been assured by her that she hadn't anything of which to be scared; so perhaps she was worrying over nothing?

ELEVEN

Almost as Louise left Robins Rest Adrian arrived at the annexe.

"I can't stay," he explained, having kissed her fondly. "I've loads of work on hand, tonight. I'm taking some home, rather than stay late at the office . . ." His laugh was rueful. "Did I say home? This is the place I regard as home: where you are, my darling . . . where we can be together."

"You could do your work here, if you liked," she offered.

"Well, two things against that," he smiled. "In the first place there isn't really enough room here; and in the second place — do I need to say it? — just how much work *would* I do? I'd want to be kissing you all the time. Have mercy on my manhood," he told her.

"Okay, then, off you go," Louise also smiled.

"I can stay a few minutes . . ." He took the girl in his arms, resting his face against the cool of her cheek. "I love you," he said, quietly. "Damn having to work! But I can't kick against it, and it's only while the firm's extra busy." He drew her close, "Please never forget me, will you?"

"I don't get much chance," Louise said. "You must phone at least twice a day."

"And I'd make it more often than that," Adrian told her, "if I weren't so damned busy. However," his mouth moved over her face leaving a series of warm kisses, "You're pleased that I love you, aren't you? And whatever you say, I do believe that in your heart you love me, Louise . . ."

She looked into his eyes, two dark pools, and while not wanting Adrian to love her too deeply, felt grateful for his affection. If she could not have Grant, as it seemed she couldn't, then maybe in time she might learn to love Adrian, instead?

Morning brought another hot Summer's day. No orders in her mail: just a letter from her father enclosing a snap of himself and Gail. 'With our new baby,' Howard had written, referring to the puppy they cuddled. "Gail has christened him Sammy,' his letter continued, "and *he* has christened just about everything we've got, as well as chewing his way through my slippers.'

Both Howard and Gail looked happy and

contented, just as Julia and Bernard also looked happy, seemed overflowing with contentment. Perhaps, after all, her parents had been right in finding true happiness elsewhere? Folk needed to make their own decisions. If convention mattered, as Louise believed it did, then it was up to herself to see she conformed; but outside her own life she had to accept that many did not share her views.

In the garden, Kim was hanging teacloths on the line. Twenty years old, the age Louise had been when Grant first became her sweetheart. She would give so much, she told herself now, to return to that evening when he'd first said he loved her, when he'd asked her to be his wife. Given a second chance — Louise heard herself sigh.

There were no second chances, were there?

Marian flashed through her mind. Louise brushed her aside; she could do without Marian's jealousy and spite; one day, she'd tell her so. She still had several tried and tested friends and must contact a few, soon. Adrian must try to accept the fact that room must be left for others, or in time they'd become too self centred.

Before starting work, Louise went to the village to collect a few items from the shops.

She had never been keen on big super markets, preferring to shop from the small general store where they knew her by name, admired her poster for the spastics, or called from the door that the soup she had asked for had come in that very morning. There were towns in plenty for those who liked them; but for Louise, walking back to Robins Rest past thatched houses with flower-filled gardens, wild roses thick in ragged hedges, there was nothing nicer than life in a country village.

Brock cycled by. He was a strongly built fellow, whose string coloured hair, insolent eyes and pasty complexion dotted over with pimples, made him distinctly unattractive. He didn't care for Louise, who had often caught him idling in the days when Eleanor Russell had employed him; and so he did no more than grunt a surly, "Morning . . ." continuing on his way without a glance.

Back at the annexe, she put her shopping away, and was about to make a coffee when Grant appeared, his long casual strides bringing him right to her door.

He had been in her mind so much these last few days, it was almost as if she had willed him to come; and now she hoped, smiling as she let him in, that things might be righted between them. Just for seconds,

Grant seemed to share her pleasure; then something vital seemed to drop from his expression. She saw him draw himself up, squaring his shoulders, as if preparing himself for an ordeal.

"I'll only stay a few minutes . . ." Adrian had said that, and it had not seemed to matter, Louise recalled; but coming from Grant, such words had the power to hurt. It made her feel that whatever he had come about had to be dealt with there and then, in as few words as needs be, she thought.

And in a way, that was true. Grant did not want to linger; he was feeling both miserable and defeated. Ever since he'd seen Louise in the other man's arms — proving Marian's words true, so to speak — Grant had told himself that the less he saw of Louise, the better it would be for them both. In his view, a break was the only solution.

His eyes, meeting Louise's bright smile, tried not to look around the level of her waist; but he longed to sweep her into his arms and to tell her that, baby or no baby, he still loved and wanted her badly.

But it was not to say all this that he had come that day; and so he said, his voice a little too tense: "I feel as if I've gone back a few years, Louise, because this is my second time of saying goodbye . . . and this time, it really *is* goodbye. I'm not trying to be dramatic . . ." He sounded choked. "I've no alternative, my dear."

There's no one else, you know! she wanted to say: But Grant was still speaking, saying bluntly: "Let's put it like this, we're not meant for each other, not as things are. That's true, isn't it?" he urged.

She looked down at his hands, now holding her own, and dared herself to betray the fact that tears were too near the surface.

"That's okay," she managed to say at last. "I don't expect you to keep coming here. Why on earth should you?" she asked.

Grant made no reply. He could have given a dozen reasons as to why he would have loved to continue to call; but only one — a very sad but definite reason — as to why he should keep away.

"So what?" Louise queried. "No use offering you a drink? A case of, 'Hallo-goodbye-and-now-close-the-friendship'? Well, great, if that's how you want it."

The old bitterness was back. She hadn't meant to speak like that. Nor had Grant intended to reply, as he did: "Don't blame me! Who was it ended things? Who sent me out of her life?"

Startled, she would not answer his questions. Only said, lightly: "Well, do we do things formally — shaking hands and wishing each other well? Or would you rather we just said cheerio and called it a day, on that?"

Grant said: "I didn't come here to bandy words. Nor am I going to drag this out, or hold an inquest on it. You know damn well why I'm having to be brief. I've simply come to say goodbye to you, Louise. So let's leave it at that, shall we?"

But why? she wanted to cry, in protest. If grief for Annabel wasn't keeping him away, then it could only be because of Adrian Pryce; yet that made no sense, at all. Surely, he wasn't walking out of her life because of that stupid little kissing scene? He didn't have any proof she was serious with Adrian; she had never told him she was.

Perched as he was on the edge of the table, and realising he still held Louise's hands, Grant slowly and reluctantly released them. It had seemed so natural to take them in his own; but facing the fact that those days when they'd been lovers were over and done with, beyond recapture, he felt he did best not to touch her.

Was there to be a child? Or had Marian Taylor been listening to rumours? he wondered. Grant knew he could not ask Louise.

But angry that he had lost her a second time, he longed to say: 'You little fool, have you reached twenty four without hearing about the pill and a dozen other methods of preventing this from happening?' Longed to say all this, but knew he could not do so, if only for the reasons that he was weeks too late and that Louise would resent being censured.

But he did say, meaning every word: "We were two fools, Louise. We had our chance four years back, and we let something very precious slip from our grasp. We must have been mad — we *were* mad! I gave in too easily; and as for you — I don't care how strongly you deny it, now — you said a hell of a lot you didn't really mean. You only thought you meant it."

Louise looked away, her eyes fixed on the window where everything seemed suddenly misted. She knew that if he asked — which he wouldn't, of course — she would go with Grant to the ends of the earth, would do anything he wanted of her, now.

But instead, he only kissed her gently, saying: "I wish you *had* loved me enough to want me. I was fond of Annabel: she was very sweet and she was beautiful, and she made me extremely happy. But you know where my heart often was, don't you? I had an awful job to forget you. I came to terms with it, yes, and my marriage was a good one; though no thanks to you that I was happy."

She wanted to say: I *did* love you, Grant! But she could only mumble: "I had a thing against marriage. I couldn't believe it would last and I wasn't going to take any chances."

"And now?" Head averted, Grant avoided her eyes, until pressing a quick parting kiss on her cheek. "I'll go . . ." His voice was husky. "Be happy," he told her. "Take it from me, marriage can still be wonderful."

Louise whispered, "Goodbye . . ." and as Grant left the annexe, Kim appeared at the bottom of the steps.

"Oo-h, Miss, I am sorry!" The girl stood back. "I didn't know you had company," she told Louise. "Is it all right to come in?"

"Yes, of course . . ." Louise choked on a smile. She had promised herself she could weep when Grant had gone; but Kim's arrival forced her to keep herself steady, which perhaps was as well, she acknowledged. She kept her voice pleasant, for it was not Kim's fault that she, Louise, had made a mess of her life by sending Grant into Annabel's arms. Besides, something about Kim's strange golden eyes told Louise that something was wrong; the girl was aching to speak, she told herself, and yet was afraid to do so.

Her own troubles temporarily pushed aside, she said, endeavouring to sound encouraging: "Is something bothering you? You look miserable, Kim." She, too, felt miserable but dared not show it. "Can you talk to me about it?" she asked.

Kim shook her head. "Nothing's gone wrong. I dunno why I came," she hedged. "I've plenty do do — I ought to be finishing the ironing."

She stood, a helpless pathetic being, twisting her fingers as she gaped at Louise. "No, nothing's gone wrong," she repeated. And in a way, nothing had, except she still felt uneasy, but knew she must not mention that frightening letter however apprehensive she felt. She had given her word; but how Kim wished, now, that there was someone in whom she could safely confide, who could put her mind at rest. It was the secrecy of it all that worried the girl: that, and the strange way the letter was addressed, and the funny glint in Miss Taylor's eyes — a cruel sort of glint, Kim reflected. She had said it was a joke she was having with someone; but there had only been evil in Miss Taylor's laugh . . .

"Something *has* gone wrong!" Louise insisted.

"Not really . . ." Kim shook her head, fiercely. "I mustn't stay," she protested. "I've been a bit lazy, this morning. But I'm glad it's keeping fine for the garden fete; I might go along, meself, later . . ."

Louise did not detain her. Her own turbulent mind seemed overflowing with the painful memory of Grant's sad farewell. If only he had kept away! she thought. She had not asked him to come. The desire to weep was still with her; but her old cynicism, fighting back, was holding the tears at bay. She did not want Grant! she told herself. Not Grant, nor any man, come to that. Certainly, she did not want love and marriage; it never worked out, anyway.

Having put her workroom ready for an afternoon's painting, she wrote to her father acknowledging his letter and making suitable comments about the puppy. The snap she framed and stood by her bed: a poor substitute for Grant's photo which she resolutely put out of sight. Her bedroom was attractive and deliberately feminine because she liked to be surrounded by beautiful things; though was there any emptier object in the whole world, she thought, than a three foot divan in a small

silent room, waiting for its one lonely oc-
cupant?

Twelve

The thought of lunch choked her, but she managed an omelette followed by fruit and a coffee. Something told her she would not do much painting, now; but she roused herself to pick some marigolds, enough to fill a bowl for her kitchen table, like bringing sunshine into the house.

She had hardly finished arranging the flowers when someone came to the door. It wasn't Adrian's ring, nor Eleanor's, nor Kim's; and sadly, it wasn't Grant's, either, for she knew all these by heart. The girl she encountered was no one she knew and her face was distinctly hostile.

"I'd like to come in," she said, coldly. "You and I are due for a talk, Miss Mackenzie. You *are* Miss Mackenzie, I take it?"

"I certainly am — and, yes, do come in." Though there were more friendly ways of requesting an entry than the method this girl had chosen. Who was she? Not a client.

Some new, unfriendly neighbour?

Standing back, Louise allowed her visitor to enter. Not much more than thirty, she seemed an ordinary girl: neither beautiful nor plain, yet in her own way attractive — or could be when less aggressive. Her dark brown hair was nicely permed, the oval shaped face devoid of make-up except for a touch of pink lipstick and the palest of eye shadow.

She refused to sit down, but came straight to the point, telling Louise: "I'm Hilary Pryce . . . Adrian's wife, Miss Mackenzie."

The room seemed suddenly to lose shape. Louise felt her colour ebb as she answered: "I'm sorry, I don't understand."

"Well, I do!" came the blunt reply. "And if you're wondering why I'm here, then read this. It might jog your memory a little." She took a letter from her bag, holding it a moment, seeming in some almost macabre way to enjoy the sudden tension in the atmosphere before passing it over to Louise. "I received this yesterday afternoon," she said. "Don't get funny and tear it up, Miss Mackenzie, because I've had a photostat taken."

"I still don't understand . . ." But Louise took the letter. It was awkwardly composed of words and letters cut out from magazines, but its meaning was all too plain.

122

'Did you know,' it said, 'that your husband, Adrian Pryce, has been visiting a Miss Louise Mackenzie all the time you have been away? She lives at The Annexe Robins Rest Millstead. He has been seeing her almost every night and sometimes takes her out in his car.'

Louise felt herself tremble as the words hit her. The first time she had seen an anonymous letter, she could hardly believe it was connected with herself, it seemed so cruel and spiteful. She began to feel slightly sick.

Bad enough that Adrian should have done this to her, lying and saying he was unmarried; but that someone should have sent this letter to his wife, made the situation grotesque.

For a moment, she could not get her lips to move. Then: "I wasn't aware he was married," she blurted. "I'm sorry — that's all I can say."

"Well, if you're short of words, I'm not," she was told. "I go away to nurse my sister who's been very ill, and this is what happens in my absence. Don't try kidding me you thought Adrian was a bachelor, it just won't wash, Miss Mackenzie."

"I did *not* know he was married," Louise repeated. "I'm not that hard up for masculine company that I have to go after someone's husband. I'm sorry, but I'm not to blame, and you'll have to believe that's so."

All the time she was speaking, her heart thumped madly, leaving her short of breath. Only the previous day, Adrian had repeatedly said he loved her, making her believe that everything he'd sworn was the truth. Even though she had known she could not return his love, at least she believed his affection to be genuine. It hadn't struck her she was being used as a stop-gap throughout the weeks his wife was away.

Not surprisingly, she felt angry and affronted. She looked at Hilary Pryce and felt helpless. She wanted to tell her again that she was sorry, even longed to say that the letter was a lie — except that it wasn't, of course. She could understand this girl would be upset. She'd been justified in thinking Adrian would stay faithful — though did anyone ever stay faithful? Louise thought, feeling a surge of bitterness. It was as if, through Adrian, she had finally proved her point.

Hilary Pryce broke the silence by saying with a sneer: "So I'm supposed to let it all go at this, am I? Write it off as something that happens in every marriage, so why not mine, as well? Perhaps it does; perhaps there's been a lot of this during the five years I've been Adrian's wife; but I can tell you this, it's the last time so far as I'm concerned."

"That's for you to decide. I'd feel the same," Louise owned. Then wished she'd kept silent as the other girl said:

"Thank you very much for your sympathy! I didn't come here asking for pity, or understanding. How dare you tell me how *you* would feel! You aren't his wife, so how the hell would you know?"

Louise remarked, speaking scathingly now: "What makes you imagine — if I *were* guilty, which I'm not — that I'd be crazy enough to think I could steal your husband? Don't you know that, apart from exceptional circumstances, the wife is always the winner?"

Though that wasn't strictly true, was it? Louise thought. Bernard's first wife wasn't, for one. She threw the thought aside, saying instead: "Someone's making trouble. If you've got any sense you'll destroy that letter and forget you ever had it."

"As easily as that?" Hilary lit a cigarette with fingers that were slightly unsteady. "You should be running a marriage guidance clinic, Miss Mackenzie. I can just see you telling all those wronged wives to love and forgive their erring husbands — you don't have many standards, do you? My husband comes here evening after evening — I won't ask for what purpose, you know best about that — after which, I'm supposed to welcome him back as if he were a hero, is that it?"

"I repeat — someone is making trouble."

"And it wouldn't be you, the person who encouraged him would it?"

Louise said: "I'm not going down on my knees to beg forgiveness for something I didn't consciously do. I've told you I'm sorry; I've also said till I'm weary that I didn't know Adrian was married. As a final reassurance, let me make it plain that I definitely don't want to see him, again, not now or at any time. Your quarrel, Mrs Pryce, is with Adrian, not with me. Now will you please go home and leave me in peace; and in future, keep your eye on your man if he strays that easily," she ended.

"Men don't stray unless they're encouraged," Hilary said. She seemed sworn to carry this battle to the finish, hatred in every sentence. "It takes two to make a bargain," she told Louise. "Two to get into bed, together."

"Listen!" Louise was furious, now. "Don't you dare —" she began, but Hilary Pryce had already burst into tears.

"He's a cheating bastard and you're nothing but a slut!" she all but yelled at Louise. "Now that I've learned what's been happening, I don't want him; and what's more, I'll get a divorce. You've seemed to find him fascinating enough to invite him here — yes, you have! — so let's see how you like him as a husband, Miss Mackenzie, because I'm finished, I'm not going on. You can have him — and I hope you give each other hell!"

Louise stood her ground. "Why the blazes," she said, "can't you believe me, Mrs Pryce? Please get out. I've had enough of your accusations."

Hilary rose. "Very kind of you," she sneered, "to give me my marching orders. I bet you *still* plan to meet him on the sly! What makes me really mad," she fumed at Louise, "is the calm way you stand pleading innocence. If you aren't the co-respondent, then for God's sake what are you? A nun teaching him his rosary?"

"I think you'd better cool down," Louise began; but got no further, for Hilary Pryce had lunged forward to hit the girl's face with a volley of hard slaps. The blows were delivered with such force that Louise was sent spinning against the wall, almost blinded with pain. The panic button was at hand, but she would not use it. Not for anything on earth would she have Kim know she'd been mixed up in a brawl.

But she was livid, now. "You do that again, and you'll regret it!" she threatened. "That's assault, Mrs Pryce. Get out of my house, or I'll call the police, do you hear me?"

"I'm going . . . don't worry!" Hilary made for the door, turning to have the last word. "Do you think I'd want to stay in this brothel of a place one minute longer than I need?"

She was gone and Louise burst into tears. Both hands to her face, as if to soothe the burning pain, she tried to rack her tired brain, querying who could have sent that letter — even wondering if more might follow. Was it someone who had spied on the annexe? she wondered. Some person who had watched Adrian's every movement — even her own, come to that? Her mind whirled back to the figure in the bushes; on each of the two occasions she'd seen it, Adrian had only just left her home — that alone roused her suspicion. She had supposed it might be Brock waiting for Kim, but now she was not so sure.

The anonymous letter had made her feel ill. Just as well Adrian wouldn't be calling, that evening; she never wanted to see him, again.

She tried to put him from her mind. Mrs Pryce, too. But the shock was still there and nothing could stop her from going over the whole sordid business from the evening Adrian had answered her advert, to his wife's visit, that day. What a fool she had been not to question him more fully; had she done so, she might easily have caught him out. Or could she? Men who indulged in affairs had all the answers beforehand.

Yet his very reticence should have made her suspicious. That carefully worded, 'No wife, I promise you . . .' Said tongue in cheek, but still a lie because he *did* have a wife, only she happened to be absent just then. She could quote a dozen lies — white, grey or black — with which he might have felt he'd cleared himself, considering them a half truth of sorts. He wasn't doing overtime several times a week. The fact was, his wife had returned home; and Adrian, who could not now be out every night, was dividing his time between them both.

Well, at least she now knew him for what he was. And the awful part was, had Grant not reappeared, she might even have grown fond of Adrian Pryce, for loneliness was an inducement and she had found him attractive. But Grant, whom she had never been able to forget, quashed all likelihood of her falling in love with Adrian.

Louise went to the bathroom and bathed her face. Grant's farewell visit . . . Hilary's attack . . . no wonder she felt a wreck. She kept away from Kim all afternoon, was glad that Eleanor did not look in. They frequently let several days go by without seeing or phoning each other, at all; so just as well, Louise decided, to make this one of those patches. She lay down for an hour, made some coffee and put all her painting away.

She was wondering how early she could go to bed, when Adrian himself arrived. Having tapped the door, he walked straight in, and before Louise could speak had her in his arms, seeking her mouth to kiss her.

"Don't!" In a fury, she wrenched herself free. "Keep that for your wife," she told him.

Adrian's face blanched. He seemed suddenly to sag, as if all the strength had been sapped from his limbs. "Oh, my God . . ." His voice sounded parched.

But he pulled himself together, forcing a smile. "Darling, what's this?" he asked.

Louise looked at him, coldly. Looked into his eyes and saw him for what he was, a cheat. Contempt made her hate him.

"In the first place, I'm not your darling,"

she returned. "And in the second place, if you haven't yet heard the news that's already floating around, then let me tell you that you soon will. And in the third place, if this needs to be said, I don't want you here today, or ever. Now please get out!" she ordered.

Adrian did not get out. He flopped into a chair and stared, bewildered, at her. "What are you on about?" he asked. "It's obvious you've somehow found out the truth; now, of course, you despise me for it. I can understand that — but please, Louise, whatever you've heard and no matter what you think, I *do* love you, truly I do. We've got to talk this over . . . we must!"

"There's nothing to discuss." Louise stayed cool. "Save your breath for when you talk things over with your wife. Believe you me, you'll have a job to justify yourself, but that's your problem, not mine."

"It need not be anyone's problem," he said, "— not if we face the truth. You're angry and upset and I can't blame you. But then neither can *I* be blamed if I love you. Who told you I was already married?"

"Who do you think?"

"Not Hilary, for God's sake?"

"Of course, who else?" Louise countered. "She paid me a visit this afternoon. Some-

131

one sent her an anonymous letter."

Adrian's mouth went taut. Temper or fear? "What was in it? I must know, Louise."

"Just what you'd expect. That you'd been coming here at night — all very exaggerated, of course. But why ask? You'll be given it, yourself, pretty soon . . . plus your wife's comments, as a bonus."

"What did you say when she showed you the letter?"

"That I was sorry, I didn't know you were married. That was the truth," Louise defended. "After all, I *didn't* know, did I? She didn't believe me — most people wouldn't; she was also mighty abusive." Louise didn't tell Adrian that Hilary had hit her. But: "You'd better prepare yourself for a scene. And what I said just now still goes," she said. "I never want to see you, again."

Adrian stared, his face contorted with shock; but she went on: "Can't you understand how rottenly you've treated us both? You've lied and cheated — and, yes, you *have* been unfaithful."

He got up to face her, shouting now. "No, I can't and won't get out of your life! And you mustn't hate me . . . you mustn't! What I feel is totally genuine, Louise. I knew it from the moment I first saw you; I can't just throw you over as if you were some cheap pick-up."

"Well, believe me, that's how your wife views me; and by the time she's finished, it's what everyone who knows me will think. And it's wholly unfair!" Louise protested. "It was you who forced the pace, and I can see why, now — you had to cash in while you could," she ended.

"Louise!" he begged, but she was keeping her distance, knowing that if Adrian tried to touch her she would fight him physically, now. "I don't particularly want any man," she told him. "Certainly not another woman's husband, so please do as I say and leave me."

"Look, I've a right to state my case," Adrian said. "I'll go, if that is what you want me to do, but I've got to explain things, first. As Hilary no doubt told you, she's been nursing her sister, and maybe I did feel lonely. Even so, it never once crossed my mind to start looking around, but then I met you, my darling . . ." He sounded full up. "No one can help falling in love. I know I should be ashamed to say this, but you're the one I love, Louise. I knew that if I owned up to being married, you would promptly blow the whole thing apart, the same as you're threatening, now."

"I'm not just threatening, I mean it."

"Then you're bloody cruel," he said, tears filling his eyes. "Look, I've got to face Hilary over this and there are going to be a good many hard words spoken. I'll get through if I know I can be sure of your love. Darling, can't we be loyal to each other?"

"For heavens sake, don't bring loyalty into this!" Louise turned aside. "You don't know the meaning of the word."

"I do — and I'll prove it to you," he said. "Do you think I've enjoyed this deceit? Between having to account for all those days when I visited Hilary and her sister at Ipswich — and then when she decided to come home! You can't imagine how I felt going to fetch her: pretending to be pleased to have her back, when all the time it was you I wanted."

"What a charming husband!" Louise remarked. "Your wife received that letter yesterday, she says. How come she hasn't shown it to you?"

"I don't know," Adrian said, "But it does explain things, a bit. She was very loving when I brought her home; but last night, she was moody and would hardly speak."

Louise preferred not to picture the scene. A fresh fear was filling her mind. If his wife *were* to start divorce proceedings, what a laugh for people like Marian Taylor — even her own parents. And after all she'd said on the subject of divorce, even Grant might raise his eyebrows.

She glanced to where Adrian was standing, waiting, his eyes begging love, forgiveness, compassion; and marvelled she had ever even liked this man, let alone wished she could love him. Whatever feelings she had once had, she wanted now to be rid of him, forever.

"I'll go . . ." He sounded on the verge of tears. "But I'll say it, again: *I love you!* Given the choice of every woman in the world, it would still be you — no one else!"

THIRTEEN

The ghastliness of everything that had happened that day went with Louise throughout the night, leaving her completely exhausted. She rose to face a day she virtually dreaded, for she couldn't imagine how she would cope if Hilary Pryce were to show up, again, nor what she would say if Eleanor became curious. Of Grant, she dared not think; he'd made their parting so definite, that to her it was more like an illness.

Louise did not accept Adrian's statement that his preference lay with herself; it stood to reason that if the crunch really came, he would panic at the thought of losing his wife and, thoroughly contrite, would beg her forgiveness.

To the girl's dismay, he rang quite early; and since the outcome of this business might well concern herself, she needed to know what was going on and was therefore compelled to listen.

Adrian said he was surprised that Hilary had said nothing either about the letter, or Louise. "She seems playing a waiting game," he said. "I'm finding it a bit unnerving. She's very withdrawn and huffy with me; and I think I'm meant to ask what the trouble is, but I'm not going to do that, Louise. Nor am I telling her I know about the letter, or she'll twig I've been to see you, again. That sounds deceitful, but the point is I need time to make plans . . . to get my finance sorted out . . . so that when the break comes, I can walk out with everything tied up and settled."

"Well, that's up to you and nothing to do with me." Louise felt as chilly as she sounded. "It's none of my business, Adrian."

"It *is* your business," he put in. "If Hilary doesn't mention divorce, I propose to launch the subject, myself, and to ask her to give me my freedom. Oh, I'm not afraid of telling her about you, Louise; I just want time to see how I'm placed."

"I can tell you how you're placed," Louise informed him. "When the letter does get mentioned, you'll cave in and, true to your sex, put the blame on me. The woman tempted me, and so on. Beyond that, you don't have to worry; because, once you've made things up, all that's left for you to do

137

is to forget me. The same as I intend to forget you . . . and the sooner the better," she said. "Do you mind if I ring off? I'm busy."

"Yes, I *do* mind! This is important, Louise. You see, Hilary must have somewhere to live; but the bungalow still has a mortgage on it, so I don't know how I'm placed about that. There's also the money, such as we have; I understand she's entitled to claim half of that. Even the car is half hers," he said. "We went shares in everything, Louise."

"Why are you telling me all this?" she asked.

"Because I want to marry you!" he said. "You're hurt with me, at present, but once we're together I know we can be happy, Louise. We've proved that . . . we've had some wonderful times since we met."

She let a sigh reach his ears, like a small tired wave. "Listen, Adrian . . ." Even her voice felt weary. "All that is finished and done with. Illicit love affairs just don't appeal! I've heard all I need and I'm ringing off, now. If you phone again, I shall put the receiver down."

His protests increased, but she did as she threatened; life was going to be difficult for awhile. She'd be constantly afraid that either

Adrian or Hilary would be ringing her doorbell, trying to get in; and then there would be the added fear of being involved in a divorce.

Several times that morning, she found herself wondering if she would perhaps be wiser to move. She hated the thought of leaving the annexe. But it was no use her staying if Adrian and his wife intended, each in their own different ways, to make life a misery for her. It seemed cowardly to contemplate moving from Millstead, but she wasn't going to stay where she wasn't happy, or where she was constantly on edge.

Yet to move would cause an upheaval in her life. She had got herself cosily dug in, her little business nicely established. She was within driving distance of both parents, was fond of Eleanor, and had taken it for granted she would be at the annexe for a good many years, yet. It would be difficult to find a similar place. Any flat, however nice, could well not suit; since so long as she worked she needed the right surroundings where she could have a studio.

Once or twice, she had toyed with the idea of getting in touch with Grant; even to ask his advice. But she got no further than thinking about it, knowing that her pride and a fear of his reaction made her shy at the very idea. It might be he could put her mind at rest by telling her that Hilary had no case, but he would still know what had happened. He had already witnessed that embarrassing scene when Adrian had been more passionate than usual. To have him know the man was married would be the last straw. No, definitely, she could not consult Grant.

Eleanor came over. "I'm not seeing much of you. Haven't you been well?" she asked. "You don't look all that good — you're not working too hard, I hope? Have lunch with me," she coaxed. "I've cooked enough for three, so you must come and join me, now . . ."

Louise accepted with a smile. Feeling as she did, her own company could only depress her. Kim ate in the kitchen; liked to do so because, as she carefully explained: "Me manners ain't all that good." This suited Eleanor. "It isn't that I'm snobbish; but what in the world could we talk about?" she asked. "By the way, did I tell you that Brock Seymour has started chasing after Kim, again? I'm sure she doesn't want him, or any other boy; though I think she likes to feel she excites him enough to keep him on his toes, so to speak."

Louise remarked: "I still can't decide

whether it *was* Brock I saw in the garden. I've not seen anyone around, lately; but on those two occasions I was quite sure, then, that there was someone hiding up."

Eleanor pulled a face. "Mercy," she said, "you'll have my nerves in shreds before you're through. I saw an advert offering Alsatian puppies in the *Eastern Daily*, yesterday morning. Do you think we ought to buy half a dozen and share them out between us?" Though she laughed, there was a thoughtful look on her face. "Brock's been a nuisance," she declared. "It was a mistake having him here to work; but there you are, he couldn't get a job. Of course, when he did find regular employment, Robins Rest simply went to the wall; he didn't even give notice. I must say the gardener wasn't sorry; Brock wasn't exactly an asset."

A pause, while Eleanor sliced through a tart, putting a wedge on each of two plates, then: "All the same, Brock mustn't walk in and out as if he's still one of us, must he?"

Louise said, no, he mustn't, then fell silent. None of this answered the question in her mind, which asked: *Was* it Brock Seymour she'd seen, or someone spying on Adrian?

Grant Sullivan, seated at his large desk,

looked down on the steady stream of traffic gliding along Angel Hill — where angels would for sure fear to tread, he thought, or they'd end in the accident ward.

At his elbow, the telephone started ringing. Grant picked it up and recognised the voice.

"That's Marian, isn't it?" He frowned as he spoke.

"That's right . . ." She gave a seductive giggle. "Just an enquiry, Grant."

"Which is?"

"Well, don't sound so off!" she said. "An invitation, that's all." A second giggle, then: "Any excuses as to why you shouldn't come along to my place for a small get-together, tomorrow night? Or do I have to *drag* you from your flat? — which I shall, if you don't soon come!"

"I'm afraid you're unlucky, Marian," he told her. "I'm not really in the mood, yet awhile. Not for that sort of thing, you know."

"Well, since you've never been to my place," she argued, "how can you say whether or not you'd have occasion to object, huh?"

"Well, cross out the word *object,*" Grant answered. "It's simply that I don't feel sociable, Marian. I'd rather be left to simmer for a time. I'm sure you understand."

She didn't, of course. Grant let out a sigh. He could hardly tell this girl he didn't want her company; though anyone else would get the message, he imagined, so why couldn't *she* take the hint?

"Just a few of us," she was saying. "Nothing rowdy, Grant. Well, you ought to know me, by now . . ."

That was the trouble, he did know her. He also knew he would be the only guest, for the very simple reason no one else would be invited; but Grant wasn't having any. "Look," he tried to sound pleasant, but at the same time firm, "I'm sorry, but I'm up to my neck in work and I've no time to talk, Marian. Thank you all the same, but —"

"The answer is, no," she supplied. "That's okay . . . some other time, maybe, Grant? Just the two of us would be rather nice . . ."

He wouldn't answer that. Only asked her to excuse him, his goodbye short, almost curt. One of these days, Grant told himself, she would learn to leave him alone.

His diary reminded him that in ten minutes time he had an appointment with a Mrs Hilary Pryce. It was marked 'urgent' and as he was free he rang his secretary to enquire if the lady had by any chance arrived.

"She's been here five minutes," the girl

said. "Shall I bring her in, Mr Sullivan?"

"Yes, do that," Grant said. A new client to the firm, he gave the young woman a welcoming smile and saw that she was comfortably seated.

Well dressed, around thirty, was how he saw her, and noticed she looked worried and miserable. So much so, he was horribly afraid she might even burst into tears.

She began by explaining that she wasn't familiar with the etiquette surrounding Grant's profession; so was it all right, she wanted to know, if she consulted him instead of the solicitor with whom her husband had dealings?

Grant smiled. "Well, you can consult whom you please," he said. "Most husbands and wives use the same firm, of course, unless —" He paused, not quite sure of himself, but Hilary had already nodded.

"Exactly . . ." Faint colour ran into her cheeks; her small mouth quivered as she spoke. "I think — in fact, I'm sure — I have grounds for a divorce. I badly need advice," she murmured.

Grant doodled with his pencil on the corner of a pad to give her a chance to compose herself. "Would you like to talk to me about it?"

She swallowed. "Well, our marriage has

been happy enough. At least, it *was* happy until I went away to nurse my sister," she explained. "I was gone four weeks, all told. I've now discovered that during this time my husband has been going to a girl's house most nights; also, that he's taken her out in our car, which is half mine, anyway." She let a few seconds pass to push the fringe from her forehead. "I know divorce is a horrible word," she said, "but I can't share my husband with another woman — and how am I to know, since he's strayed this time, that he isn't always going to stray, or may already have done so, before?"

Grant said: "Well, let's keep to the present, shall we? Do you have the name of this girl, or woman? And do you have reliable evidence? One has to be very careful, you see, not to confuse friendship with adultery; one mustn't make false accusations. On the other hand, if during your absence your husband has actually been sleeping at her house — especially with no one there, but themselves — well, that's a different story."

"But you don't *have* to wait until bedtime, do you? Not for that, I mean?" Hilary felt a fool. What she meant, only she wasn't going to say it outright, was that there was no hard and fast rule about the act. Not a case of only between dusk and dawn, and never anywhere except in a bed; people did it all over the place.

She tried again, and Grant felt sorry for her. "What," she asked, "if they both deny adultery? I mean, how the hell can one prove it?"

"We'll get round to that in a minute," he promised. "You say you have proof he's been visiting this person. May I ask who told you this?"

"I had a letter, an anonymous one," she said, beginning to search in her bag. "I was watering the plants in my lounge, on Monday, when a girl came up the path and put something through my door. I didn't take a great deal of notice of her, because I thought she was delivering circulars — you know? But I got the impression that she was rather dumpy, with an awkward sort of walk and sandy hair. Later, I found this letter on the mat . . ." Hilary shook her head. "Damn, I've left it at home. Will it be all right for me to bring it in, tomorrow?"

Grant nodded. "Did you show the letter to your husband?"

"No, I thought I'd get advice, first. I've pretended I've not felt very well, so we've not slept together since I had this letter; he must be thinking I'm pregnant, the way I keep saying I feel sick and have a headache," she said. "Also, I've got to be honest, Mr Sullivan, I haven't felt very friendly towards him; we're only just on speaking terms."

"Hasn't he asked what's wrong?"

"No, he hasn't, not yet. And as I say, I haven't mentioned the letter."

"Well, he ought to be allowed to read it," Grant said, "and given a chance to explain to you why he's been going to this house. Or even if he went as often as this letter implies. It could have come from someone with a warped, unpleasant mind — believe you me, such people do exist by the thousands — in which case, Mr Pryce could be innocent. Why don't you let him read it for himself and then see what he has to say?"

"He'll only deny it, the same as she did. People mostly lie when they're cornered."

"Have you been to see this woman, then?"

"Yes — yesterday afternoon. She feigned innocence, of course; didn't know he was married; all that sort of talk, which I didn't believe. I suppose she didn't want to be cited as co-respondent, though that still doesn't put her in the right. I wouldn't feel so hurt," Hilary said, "had I been a rotten wife to Adrian. But he didn't have to marry me, Mr Sullivan — I never chased him, or anything like that. I'm just an ordinary person, very average," she said, shaking the start of tears away, "but I've always done my best and I truly thought everything was fine between us."

"And it probably is," Grant assured her, but already the tears had won. Hilary dipped her head, furious with herself. To cry in front of a perfect stranger! Chewing at her lip, she kept her head averted while she dived into her bag for a fresh hanky. Then: "Oh, look . . ." She spoke against the thickness of tears. "I did bring the letter, after all!"

Grant put out a hand. "Oh, yes, typical," he said. "Nothing written by hand — every word cut from a magazine, or newspaper — not a pretty sight, in fact, very nasty."

He took the letter from its envelope and, starting to read, felt as if he, too, had been attacked. Each word brought pain, like the cut of a whip; Grant felt transfixed with horror. 'Did you know your husband . . . Miss Louise Mackenzie . . . almost every night . . .' He put the letter down, stifling the need to cry out. And while Hilary endeavoured to conquer her tears, he himself was fighting his own emotions, pretending to think on what he had read until he dared speak aloud.

And all the time, crystal clear in his

mind's eye, he was getting a play-back of Louise and her lover locked in their embrace: . . . in their lovers' kiss . . .

It made him feel his heart would break.

But *was* that Pryce he had seen? Grant asked himself. Adrian Pryce had been named in the letter; but on such a short acquaintance, no matter how amorous, how could Louise be certain she was pregnant, as Marian Taylor had insisted? Unless she had known Pryce even longer than the writer of the anonymous letter was aware? — though even that didn't really make sense. Because according to Marian Taylor, a wedding had been fixed; and how could Adrian Pryce offer marriage to Louise, since this man was already married?

Either he was posing as a bachelor, or widower, or some other man was involved. Confused, Grant shook his head. He felt angry, now: angry with Louise, with the whole sordid world — even with himself, for caring. Well, someone, somehow, had to sort all this out; and one thing was certain, it would not be himself. He had neither the stamina, nor courage. This must be someone else's pigeon . . .

Even so . . . Grant drew himself up in his chair. Mrs Pryce had composed herself, now, he saw. He put the letter aside and heard her say:

"What do *you* think, Mr Sullivan?"

FOURTEEN

Hilary sat in her pinewood kitchen staring at the cup of tea she had made. She didn't want it but there was something in the female chemistry which always sent them flying to the kettle and teapot the moment something went wrong.

She drank a sip or two, then poured the remainder down the sink; it tasted foul, like fur on her tongue. She felt at loggerheads with the whole world, that day; even with her sister for being ill, so that Hilary had been away long enough for Adrian to get into mischief.

She lit a cigarette. It did better than the tea, since at least she could draw on it, savagely, while pacing the kitchen floor. "I hate Adrian!" she stormed. "He's a swine!" she told the four walls. "And that girl is nothing but a dirty little trollop! I wish I'd done more than just slap her face; I should really have set about her . . ."

That morning, she had purposely baited Adrian by sneering as he left for work. His guilty eyes had lowered as he'd asked: "What's got into you this morning, then?" Adding: "You're not well, are you?"

She laughed at that, an artificial laugh, baring her teeth at Adrian. "Another one," she'd scoffed, "who's pretending to be innocent! How deceitful can you get? You must think I'm blind, deaf and crazy! However . . ." She had managed to sound indifferent. "If you're late home, tonight, I shall quite understand. Remember me to the girl friend, won't you?"

Adrian had kept silent, refusing to answer, his closed mouth surly now. It had driven Hilary to add to her sneers, even to tell him she had met Louise Mackenzie, not caring if this did make him jump.

"I can see why you're in love with her," she'd said, sweetly. "She looks a nice sexy little piece — is she? Just the sort you men would go for! Now don't say you've only seen her the once. Read this — it makes very interesting news. You can't deny things, now, can you?"

Until then, he had kept his head averted; but at the mention of the letter Adrian had turned and snatched it out of her hand. "That's only the photostat," she had said, "the original is locked away, safe!" She hadn't told him she'd got Rosalie to photostat the letter — Rosalie, who had begged her not to be impulsive, but who had nevertheless done as she had asked.

Had Rosalie not obliged, she would have asked Marian Taylor, who seemed the sort to help anyone in trouble. A real good neighbour, was Marian.

When Hilary had returned from the shops on Monday, Marian had stopped her. "Nice to see you around, again! I was sorry about your sister — is she better?"

At that point, it had been good to be home; and people like Marian, Hilary decided, made it all the nicer because they'd been pleased to see her. Later, after receiving the letter, she'd felt tempted to run to Marian for comfort, certain she could trust her, implicitly. But in the end, Rosalie had persuaded her against it, which perhaps was as well since anonymous letters were not for everyone's eyes . . .

When she'd thrust it into Adrian's hand, that morning, her own had shook like a palsy.

He had been furious, asking: "What the devil?" as if she had written it, herself. "I only went to get a portrait done of Fritz," had been his excuse as he flung the letter down. "If I stayed and talked awhile, that wasn't a crime, was it?" Yes, he'd had to go back a second time, because the first photo wasn't suitable, he'd said. And then he'd gone a third time to fetch the finished portrait. So what was all the hoo-ha about?

"Then why did she lose colour when I said who I was? And why did you keep going to her place?" she had asked. "Was this *also* to discuss Fritz's protrait? Miss Mackenzie makes mighty heavy going of her work if it necessitates all these visits!"

She would not cry in front of Adrian, not she! He'd have known, then, how upset she was. Instead, she'd adopted a don't-care stance and had purposely kept her voice cool, as if she were acting in a play. Then he'd said it: "All right, I *did* go pretty often and I liked her very much," he had owned. Adrian's thick eyebrows had drawn together, a sign that he was either angry or distressed. "But I'm not discussing it," he had told Hilary, "Why start all this just as I'm due to leave?"

She'd have felt less upset had he point-blank denied that he'd been there more than the three occasions originally mentioned by him. But now he'd admitted he'd been 'pretty often', which could have meant every evening. She still wouldn't cry, but had shouted at him: "Go to work, then, and good riddance to you! You've never loved me, or you wouldn't have been unfaithful! You wouldn't care —" this, as he'd reached the hall, "— if you came home and found me dead," she told him. "I believe you'd *like* to see me dead! You could shack up, then, with that tart of yours. Well, go to her as soon as you like, do you hear me? And don't ever come near me, again . . ."

No, she hadn't cried while Adrian was around; but now her tears fell lavishly, washing her cheeks with their warm comforting saltness. "I hate him!" she wept, feeling savage. "I wish we had never met."

Hunched, now, on a stool, she gave herself up to going through the years she'd been married to Adrian: picking it all over, searching for flaws and stubbornly refusing to call to mind all the happier times they had known. She forgot the day they'd put their first payment on the bungalow they were buying . . . forgot the fun of choosing their furniture . . . Nor would she look back on the wedding, itself . . . the honeymoon in Italy . . . the 'settling in' months . . . the nights which could never be too long . . .

But she could recall very plainly that Adrian had laughed when her first batch of scones had been underdone: that he could fly off the handle when he couldn't find something he wanted. She recalled, too, that he'd insisted on waiting instead of starting a family straighway, so that she was the only one in the Close who wasn't pushing a pram. And she remembered, too, that he'd forgotten her birthday until he'd spotted her cards in a row in the sideboard; then had dashed out and bought one to put beside them, and hadn't even said he was sorry.

Hilary flung her hanky into the wash. Her nose was stuffed up, her hair damp where she had made her head hot through crying. To make matters worse, there was Rosalie from next door ready to take her toddler to play school, before going to the office where she sometimes did part time work. When she eventually broke with Adrian she could be one of the office crowd, again, Hilary planned; but she'd see he paid maintenance, as well; she'd see him punished for what he had done.

She let the other girl in, ashamed of the fact that she had obviously been crying a lot. "I showed Adrian that letter," she mumbled. "That was the lawyer's suggestion. Adrian couldn't deny he's been seeing her; I caught him out good and proper. He as good as admitted there's been something there. I feel I hate him, now . . ."

Rosalie put her arms around Hilary. "Look, don't take this too much to heart," she begged, "or you'll end by spoiling your looks. There's nothing worse than tears and getting stirred up for playing havoc with one's face."

"Am I supposed to be laughing my head off, then?" Hilary couldn't be lectured to by someone whose husband was known by all and sundry to be faithful.

Rosalie hadn't finished. "Well, of course you're upset; this letter must have given you a ghastly shock, but you can see how things happened, Hilary. You went away — no fault of yours, because you had to go — but Adrian missed you, of course. When this girl saw how lonely he was, she led him on. Some girls are like that — they can be real bitches, worse then men, I reckon."

"I don't see this helps *me,*" Hilary said.

"No, you're right, it doesn't, of course." Rosalie's eyes seemed to ooze pity. "I know it's easy for me to talk," she owned. "I'm not the one who's hurt — and you *have* been hurt! — but this need not be the end, you know. Why don't you burn that letter?" she suggested. "Even better, laugh at the whole business and write it off as a big silly joke! Adrian adores you, Hilary, so why don't you try to forgive him?"

Rosalie drew a deep breath and put her head on one side, as if watching for a smile to break through the tears. "Show him you love him, that deep down you really trust him," she urged. "Do that, and I'm sure you can weather this patch. Only, for God's sake never refer to it, again. Say your piece, if you must; then shut up for good and start loving him like hell — okay?"

"No, it *isn't* okay!" Hilary flung back. "Is this how it will be every time I turn my back? Always *me* acting the loving, forgiving partner while Adrian goes from woman to woman? I'm not that much of a fool," she said, "I do still have *some* pride . . ."

Rosalie gone, tears flowed afresh. "Adrian's a brute and I hate him, now," Hilary said, aloud. She went on saying it. "I hate him . . . hate him . . ." Until her throat ached from the very effort and all her tears were exhausted.

FIFTEEN

As Friday dawned, the nightmare seemed
over — temporarily, at any rate. Eleanor was
spending the weekend at Braintree, and
rather than be left in the house alone at
night, Kim was to sleep at the vicarage,
though she would be at Robins Rest during
the day, just to keep an eye on the place.

With no immediate jobs on hand, Louise
planned to catch the only bus that would
take her into Sudbury, that morning. She
would browse around the shops, she promised herself, then find somewhere nice for
lunch.

Quite definitely, she needed to get out for
a while, if only for a change of scene. What
was going on in the Pryce household, Louise couldn't begin to imagine — unless, as
she suspected, they had made things up by
now. On the other hand, if they were still at
variance, would Hilary really petition for
divorce? And were these as easily obtained

as the girl seemed to believe? One person could provide the answer to that. Grant Sullivan — who else? She need not give details, Louise told herself: just ring him and say, in the course of conversation, that someone she knew thought she'd grounds for divorce. Ask what *he* made of the set-up? "You know about these things, Grant," she could say. "*Could* one sue on such slight evidence?"

But Grant was no fool. Let Louise say that, and however casually she put the question, he would know there was more to it than that. She must keep silent or come clean.

Very well, she *would* come clean! she instructed herself, and she would do so, that very minute. She could ring Grant, now, before he went to his office; and if she couldn't fix an appointment with him, then she'd simply have to gabble it over the phone. But she had to speak to him.

He had given her his number and she straightway dialled it. Already, her heart was hammering.

Grant answered at once and, hearing his voice, Louise knew she could not only *not* tell him — she was not even going to try. Instead, she mumbled: "Hallo, Grant . . . how are things, these days?"

A pause, then: "I'm fine. That's Louise,

isn't it?" Was there something just a trifle cool in Grant's reply? Not angry. Or was he? Louise felt uncomfortable.

Was he angry? Could she have seen Grant's expression, she would have known he was more upset than angered — and perhaps more hurt than upset. That Louise, of *all* people, should get herself named as the person who was after this young woman's husband, seemed beyond all belief. In view of all she'd said regarding her parents, this just made a hypocrite of her, Grant thought; and he could not bear to know that the girl he still loved should have such a tag put upon her.

Louise seemed slightly apprehensive. Grant only hoped she wouldn't ask him to act on her behalf in the event of a possible case being brought, because he couldn't act for both sides, could he? Though he wasn't going to act for Mrs Pryce, come to that; he'd already as good as passed her over to one of the firm's other partners.

Louise's nervousness made Grant nervous, too. She sounded tired and deflated, he thought. Straining his ears, he heard her say that she was only ringing to say hallo . . . that the bus she hoped to catch was almost due . . . so, forgive her, she'd have to ring off.

Well, if that was all she had to say — ? Grant shook his head, mystified, now. Why phone him at all? he wondered.

Now Louise had said goodbye and the line had gone dead; he stared at the receiver and swore. Yes, let him be honest, she still mattered to him; and whatever kind of fool she might have been, and even if she *were* pregnant by Pryce, Grant knew he was still incredibly fond of this girl he had once hoped to marry. Even when he had paid that last visit to her — ostensibly to bid her goodbye forever — his real motive had been purely and simply one more excuse to see, and be with her, again.

Well, presumably Louise knew what she was doing; and if she intended marrying Pryce once he were divorced and free to marry, Grant could only hope she would be happy. But he still could not accept that she had changed to this extent. Had she *no* regrets? None of this seemed like Louise Mackenzie. Grant wished, now, he'd kept her talking.

Several hours later, a Datsun car turned off from the traffic-filled Haverhill road into a country lane still scented with Summer flowers.

At its wheel, Adrian dropped speed, his

lips set and taut, his eyebrows drawn into a heavy and worried frown. He knew too well why he was reluctant to hurry; and if he had needed any reminding, the wooden signpost just ahead was there to explain the reason.

It stood, one finger beckoning him home . . . the second pointing to Bury St Edmunds . . . the third, urging him to turn left in the direction of Robins Rest.

For nearly thirty six hours, he had been in a turmoil; and now Adrian dreaded the weekend, ahead. Two long days in which he'd crave to be with Louise, while the hours dragged on in an atmosphere so tense he'd feel tempted to do something desperate. How would he endure it? And why was he going home, when he hated the sight of the place?

He would have to be more explicit, soon: to tell Hilary that, yes, he *did* love Louise: that it was no passing fancy.

'I'm sorry, Hilary, but I'm terribly in love . . .' Was that how he would word things? he wondered. When the moment arrived, he would not find it easy, being too afraid of Hilary's threats and tears to make her see how he felt. Were there any words, anyway, for putting it kindly? Adrian drew his car to a standstill. He tried to rehearse what he

would say to his wife — because like it or not, she *was* still his wife . . .

Adrian thought of Louise with a sudden longing. He could not understand why she had lost her head when Hilary called upon her. By admitting she hadn't known he was married, she had simply made him sound a despicable cad. Agreed, he *should* have said that he had a wife; and he would have done so, he told himself, had he not been afraid that Louise would have finished with him. Yet she knew he loved her; that knowledge, alone, should have made her sure of herself.

To find herself confronted by an outraged wife would be a shock to the calmest of girls, he supposed; but he still wished Louise had kept cool. She had only to order Hilary out; the big discussions could have waited until later when he, himself, arrived.

In any case, why talk as if they'd cause to feel ashamed? With the entire world madly swapping partners, what the devil did one more change-over matter? Louise had let him down, there.

He put the car into gear and looked at the finger which told him that Millstead was one mile away. At that moment, he could easily have wept. He had a wife who was threatening to start a divorce, and a girl who had suddenly turned against him and who wouldn't believe he loved her.

On he went. No alternative, Adrian confessed. Since Louise had forbidden him to visit the annexe, he could only obey her orders, much as it sickened him to do so. Reaching Linsell Green, all spirits dropped and he knew that, somehow, whatever the outcome, he would have to see Louise that same weekend, or go completely crazy.

The Datsun put away, Adrian let himself in; then, gasping, stood appalled at what he saw.

In the kitchen, Hilary had taken his razor and had just slashed both her wrists.

SIXTEEN

Had the milkman not chosen that moment to call, her front door would not have been wide open, allowing Adrian to walk straight in as if he owned the place.

Louise stepped back without closing the door. She had told Adrian to keep away, and she was not going to have him override her orders; though something told her there was trouble ahead.

Earlier, Louise had made up her mind that if Adrian should prove a nuisance to her, then she would ask Grant to write him a warning letter, advising him not to pester. She would feel small, making this request to Grant; but since their friendship seemed written off, now, it didn't really matter what he thought, or even what he said, come to that.

All this had flitted through Louise's mind, almost as if she had received advance news that Adrian was planning to see her. Now, meeting his dark smouldering eyes she knew something had happened to change him. Whereas once she had thought him tolerably handsome; now, suddenly, he looked a devil.

She said: "Whatever it is you have to say, will you please make it brief and then leave? You've got a nerve to come here, in any case."

Adrian waited, taking a deep breath before saying in a voice that had gone beyond rage: "You can say that, again! Hilary endeavoured to kill herself . . . I've been nearly off my head with worry." He was gulping, now, as if struggling not to weep. "She slashed both her wrists and damn near died. If she had, it would have been *your* fault!"

Louise's own voice sounded weak. "She really did *that?*"

"Yes, she really did that!" Adrian mimicked. "And in case you need telling twice," he said, "Hilary tried to take her life! I found her in the kitchen . . . blood all over the floor . . ."

Louise felt slightly unsteady. "Is she . . . is she all right?"

"She's still alive, if that's what you're trying to say." Adrian stepped closer, his eyes blazing. "What the hell do you care, anyway?" His voice had risen to a blustering shout and Louise was thankful that Eleanor was away: she would have hated her to hear this rumpus. He can't hurt you! she kept trying to console herself. No, he couldn't and wouldn't — at least, she hoped he wouldn't; though any love he'd ever felt was completely dead and he wasn't disguising the fact.

It didn't surprise her. This, she supposed, was the sort of finale she might have expected. Love turned to hate . . . lover turned enemy . . .

But she was not being blamed for any of this and certainly not for Hilary's attempt at taking her own life. From the moment she had learned that Adrian was married, she had completely and resolutely broken with him. Yes, of course, it must have been a ghastly experience for a man to find his wife with both wrists slashed; but let the blame be kept to its proper channel, not flung at herself out of spite.

Adrian said, as if speaking between clenched teeth: "It's taken until now for me to get things straight. You damn near wrecked my marriage!"

"That isn't fair, or true . . . and you know it isn't!" Louise was as enraged as himself, now. "Listen," she began, but he talked her down, almost pushing her against the wall.

"No, you listen to me," he ordered, roughly. "Let's face it, you were out to catch a lover — yes? Not a husband, you seemed to have a thing against marriage; but nothing against an escort, a lover . . . No, you didn't know I was already married — I grant you that, and I should have told you; though I doubt very much you would really have cared, either way."

"Then why was I furious when I learned the truth?"

"It wasn't the truth you minded. It was finding yourself face to face with my wife and knowing your game was up," he said. "That's what got you, Louise. As soon as I saw the way things were going, I should have finished with you. But there was no way out for me, was there?"

"What utter rubbish!" Louise put in. "You could have broken at any point."

"Could I? You know damn well I couldn't. You knew the effect you had upon me and it pleased you to see me making a fool of myself. Why the hell couldn't you have called things off? The truth is," sworn now to have his full say, he was sending the words tumbling from his mouth, "you knew you had me trapped and whatever the outcome, you weren't letting go, were you?"

"Have you finished?" Louise wanted to

know. Livid, she was quite as enraged as he. "If you spoke the truth, you would have to admit that I continually asked you to cool off, Adrian."

"Try telling that to someone else," he sneered. "In other words, being a nervous little spinster, you didn't even like me to kiss you, is that it? You never pushed me off, though, did you?"

"I'd have flung you out, had I known you were married, but you insisted you weren't," she retorted. "You lied like hell from the beginning."

Adrian said nothing. Just stared at the girl, heart thumping wildly, all words gone from his throat. His distressed mind recaptured the memory of Hilary, blood on her wrists as she sank down, crying. Between sobs, she had said over and over again: "What have I to live for? I *want* to die. Leave me, I'd rather be dead . . ."

Adrian had raced next door for Rosalie. "No, don't call a doctor," she had told him, saying: "This isn't serious, truly it isn't. Just sit down and try to calm yourself. I can easily cope, Adrian."

It was all right for Rosalie. This wasn't her tragedy. Could she not see what a near thing this was? Grasp the danger Hilary was in? He had turned on her furiously, crying as he spoke. "How dare you make light of anything so serious? Look at her wrists . . . all that blood! She'd be dead by now, if I hadn't come in when I did."

All this time, Hilary had continued sobbing; and Adrian had dropped to his heels beside her. "Please, you've got to live!" he had begged. "For my sake, you must . . . please!" Distraught, he had not ceased stroking her face, all the while praying to God. Later, he had had to apologise to Rosalie; but overnight, watching her tending his wife, bathing Hilary's wrists, applying thin strips of plaster — at that point, she had seemed so indifferent that he could easily have sworn at the girl.

The whole evening had been one traumatic experience; those minutes during which he'd been sick with grief and beset with fear lest Hilary should die, would stay with him for life, he thought, now.

And in those moments, holding her in his arms, feeling her tears warm against his cheek, he had known all too well to which girl he belonged and where it was his loyalties lay. Not with Louise, beautiful though she was; but with Hilary who had proved she could not live without him.

Now, back in Louise's little home Adrian felt so outraged, so let down, ashamed, that temper seemed almost to inspire him to kill.

He would have to get out, or he'd attack her.

"I wish I'd never set eyes upon you," he spat. And yet, looking now at this lovely girl, he knew he *had* loved her almost to distraction. Even as her clear hazel eyes met his glance, Adrian still felt the same upsurge of longing as when he had first met her.

Yes, he *had* loved Louise and that brought more guilt, because it should have been Hilary for whom he had longed; yet in all the time his wife had been away, he had scarcely given her a thought. When he said he'd been trapped, he had spoken the truth; except it wasn't Louise who had set the snare, he'd walked into it himself, uninvited.

And that was something else to bring a flush to his face: the knowledge that she, too, had spoken the truth when she'd said she would never have had him near her had she even suspected he was married. Adrian knew to his fury that struggle as he might in an endeavour to shift the blame from himself, Louise was entirely innocent.

How could one love and hate a person all in the same breath? he wondered. And how could you hate them *because* you loved them? Adrian's longing for Louise was so great at this moment, he found it hard to keep his hands from her body, even felt he could be brutal with her. And yet he loved her in a nobler way, too, one which was quite apart from sex. Just to be with her, always . . . to feel her presence . . .

But he would keep his thoughts hidden, telling her, instead: "I'm hoping, please God, to save my marriage . . . hoping in time to forget you. Maybe one day," he sounded vicious, now, "someone will break *your* heart."

She thought of Grant and knew her heart seemed already breaking; but pushed that from her mind, lifting her chin in defence. Adrian was standing very still, scarcely breathing; and inwardly she panicked lest he had it in mind to hit her, as Hilary had done. The panic button was behind her, but in Robins Rest only Kim was at home, that day. Dare she put it to use? Louise queried.

The answer was, she wouldn't; Kim was in the garden and had probably been there some time. She wasn't even within calling distance. Adrian was still staring at Louise. "I think you'd better go," she said, with meaning, "before you do something silly. If it gives you any satisfaction to know this, your wife has already slapped my face. And she did it very thoroughly, Adrian."

Still she would not panic, but walked

calmly to the door, opening it wide as she spoke. "Now will you please leave," she said, quietly. "And if you ever walk in uninvited, again, I shall regard it as trespass."

He brushed past her, tears pouring from his eyes. "Damn you!" he shouted. "Damn you . . ."

As he raced down the steps, across the drive to his car, an astonished Kim suddenly appeared carrying a punnet of raspberries. She waited until the car's door had slammed, then timidly approached Louise.

"I've been picking these, Miss," she said, primly. "Mrs Russell said to see you had some while they lasted, so I done this punnet for you. I did start to bring them over, just now, but then I heard —" She stopped, one hand to her mouth. Was this taking a liberty? she wondered.

But liberty, or not, she had to say it. "I'd give him up, if I was you," she told Louise. "It's nothing to do with me, but this is how I sees it: if he's like this, now, what the hell sort of husband would he make?"

Seventeen

Kim was right, Louise thought, she was more correct than she knew. Relief that Adrian was out of the annexe, made her feel she could breathe at last.

"They look lovely . . ." She stood the raspberries down.

"Though watch 'em," Kim advised. "They're nice, but they do need a good look-over, if you know what I mean, Miss Mackenzie?"

Louise did know. "Will do!" she laughed. She was doing her utmost to push Adrian from her mind. Just as well Kim had thought to look in, Louise decided: at least she'd taken the edge off her fear.

Over coffee, she determinedly chatted with the girl, remarking that Mrs Russell was having good weather . . . that it made a nice change for Kim to sleep at the vicarage . . . that it would soon be Harvest Sunday . . .

And then the field adjacent to Robins Rest. "They'll be cutting that on Monday," Louise remarked.

Kim sat nodding at everything Louise said. "You can smell that corn is ripe," she volunteered. "It's got a warm sort of smell, ain't it?" Without waiting for an answer, she went on, "I give Brock his marching orders, today. I told him I don't want no boys in my life. I'm all right as I am, Miss Mackenzie."

"Good for you — you certainly seem okay."

"Well, I wouldn't want Brock, no ways on," Kim said. " 'You keep creeping around Mrs Russell's drive,' I told him, 'and one of these nights she'll send for the police!' That'll stop his gallop, I reckon."

Louise all but gasped. "Did he *say* he's done that? Coming round at nights, I mean?" Then it *was* Brock she'd seen! A lot of worry all for nothing! Louise thought, though it was good to have her mind put at rest. "But what did Brock gain?" she asked Kim. "Coming late at night to lurk around the shrubs . . ."

Kim covered her mouth with two red hands. "Well, I know why he's been coming," she confessed. "You see, I sleeps round this side of the house, and thinking I wasn't on view, I never drew me blinds at night. It never struck me someone might be watching." Kim's marmalade eyes pleaded innocence. "It seems he's been coming regular, more or less, just to see me undress! He reckons he had a good view from where he stood . . . says he's seen about all of me, now." Kim looked ashamed at the very idea. "Aren't men awful!" she said.

Twenty minutes after Kim had left, the telephone started ringing. Louise jumped at the sudden interruption and for a second was almost afraid.

"Hallo . . ." Apprehensive, she did not even give her number. Only stood, certain that whoever this was must surely sense the fear in her voice.

But: "Hallo . . ." This was Grant's rich baritone coming across the wires. Strong, yet soothing, it still had the power to thrill her.

He asked: "Louise? I'd like to see you, if I may. As soon as convenient — today, if that's all right? We might even manage lunch together."

"No, I'm sorry." She was almost curt in her reply. Like Kim, she had had enough of men. "I don't feel like visitors, today." She'd had as much as she could take of the opposite sex; now she needed to relax and recover.

"Perhaps some other time," she told him.

"Like that?" She couldn't blame him for sounding peeved. "Well, phone if you change your mind."

She spent the rest of the day regretting the fact that she had spoken so hastily to Grant. At the time, it had been true that she wanted to be alone; but as time lengthened out, she changed her mind and wished she had allowed him to come.

It was warm inside the house. She moved into the garden, feeling the evening deepen around her as the last lazy twittering of birds gradually lapsed into silence. Automatically, her mind fastened upon Adrian. Go back one week and none of this had happened; she'd still been living in her little fool's paradise. She had not known that Adrian had a wife . . . the anonymous letter had not been received . . . the sun had shone with a peaceful warmth. And on that day, Louise recalled, she and Adrian had walked Southwold beach, had kissed goodnight when the time came to part . . .

And now, all over. All finished.

Eighteen

She might have known Grant would not be put off. In the morning, there he was, right on her doorstep almost as the church's calling bell ceased, his six foot two filling her doorway and blacking out the sun, more welcome than she dared tell him.

So he stood with his large reassuring smile, but taking nothing for granted until Louise invited him in. Then he reached for her hand, squeezed, and let it drop. She wished he would kiss her, but he didn't.

"I don't know if I'm welcome, or pushing in where I'm not," Grant began, "but I have to see you, Louise. We're going to sort all this out," he told her.

"Sort all what out?" She was playing for time.

"You know very well what I mean. I've had just about enough," he declared. "Broken hearted wife . . . enraged husband . . . rumours, intrigue, you name it and I've met

179

it! And to cap it all I get a flea in my ear from *you,* of all people."

"Grant, I don't want a scene." She had had enough of those.

"Neither do I," he retorted, "but why should there be any scene? All we have to do is talk things over, it's as simple as that," he told her. "Couldn't be simpler, in fact." He added, giving her a wary look: "If we can't do that after all these years, then something's gone radically wrong."

Things went wrong when I acted like a fool, Louise thought. When I chased you out of my life.

"You take first throw, then," she said.

"Very well . . ." He nodded. "Yesterday morning, I happened to pay a visit to my office — unusual on a Saturday, of course — and who should be there but a furious looking fellow, literally after my blood. He reckoned I'd been giving his wife the wrong advice. In the end, I had to tell him frankly to take his grievances elsewhere. Well, now that I'm rid of that idiot and his wife, will you kindly keep cool and tell your Uncle Grant what the devil has been going on?"

Cornered, Louise saw no alternative and in a way, she was not sorry. Adrian was a blusterer but Grant had a different kind of forcefulness, one which didn't hurt, or intimidate.

"But before I start," she said, "— you mentioned someone's husband. Do I know him, Grant?"

"Yes, I'm sorry to say you do," he told her. "Sorry, because it doesn't seem like you to get involved with a married man. I know that's none of my business, Louise; but I'll say it again — it doesn't sound like the girl I once knew."

"Well, you don't know the circumstances, do you?"

"No, I don't, and I'm not after confidences, either; so no details, please. You know I saw you with this man — that's all we need to say."

Louise talked him down. "Hold it," she said. "I think I know what's in your mind, so let me explain! I did *not* know Adrian was married. Not until a few days ago, and at that point I broke with him, Grant. After everything I've said and thought, in the past, I'm not likely to break anyone's marriage. So I don't plead guilty, there . . ."

"I'm glad of that . . ." A feeling stronger than relief made him snatch a deep breath before telling the girl: "I apologise, Louise. As you say, I misjudged you, and I ought to have known better," he said.

"Well, no doubt you had cause." But Louise was frowning. "So will there be a divorce?" she enquired. "I do have a reason for asking this, and it's not because I want the husband! In fact," she spoke anxiously, watching Grant, now, "I would much rather know they had patched things up. *Really* come together, I mean."

Grant thought for seconds, before replying: "I don't think you need worry about them." Another pause, in which he let his eyes trap her own, not quite sure what her reaction would be. "I understand they're back in each other's arms," he said, "as I'd very much like us to be, Louise! But that's a separate issue. We've some talking to do first, haven't we?"

Very willingly, she gave him the whole story, starting from the day Adrian answered her advert, to his final visit the previous morning when he had walked in, uninvited. Grant listened without asking any questions. "That's okay," he said, at last. "I accept every word. You've been completely honest with me, haven't you?"

"I've no cause to be otherwise," Louise said. "But I'm rather bothered about Hilary Pryce. I hear she slashed her wrists . . ."

"Well, forget it," Grant said. "What was needed for those cuts? — just a couple of thin strips of sticking plaster! If after that, the couple could go to bed and make love, I don't think anyone could describe what happened as a serious attempt at suicide! But the main thing is, Mrs Pryce scared her husband and it brought him to his senses and so one can say she achieved her purpose. That is the position. Good luck to them both; though I'm sorry for you, my pet . . ."

A long time since Grant had called her that. Not since those never forgotten days of ill-afforded meals, long country hikes, moderate priced seats at the cinema, and drives in Grant's little run-about car secretly referred to as the love nest.

"I'll get us a drink," she told him.

"Not for a moment . . ." He put out a hand, drawing her back. "Do you mind if we finish, now we've started? We've a few more points to cover, yet. I'm sorry, but we have," he said. "And the first is, why did you not come to see me as soon as Hilary Pryce left you? Had you done so right away, you could have beaten her to it; as things were, you very nearly got me landed with someone who was out to make a hussy of you; though I wouldn't have handled the case. I do have my limits, and like the rest I'm only human, you know . . ."

"She would still have come to you," Louise reminded him.

"Yes, Mrs Pryce would still have consulted me," he said, "but by then I'd have known the truth." He let the subject drop speaking instead of other topics and deliberately avoiding the one subject which could tie a knot in his throat. Yet there was no sense delaying it further, he supposed; and so, he captured Louise by holding her fast in his arms.

"Look at me, please . . ." His heart seemed to jolt. "I dread your answer," he said, quietly, "but it's a question I must ask . . . and you'll have to forgive me, Louise . . ."

Quite instinctively, he pressed his face against her own, turning to kiss one corner of her mouth before trusting himself to speak. Strange how time could blot out the past. Louise seemed so right, there in his embrace; it was as if she had come back to where she belonged; as if the past few years had been a dream and only this was real.

But even as he thought this, the question was back, making him fearful of her answer. Grant felt his jaw tighten, heard his breathing quicken as the words flew out, asking Louise:

"This need not make any difference . . . but *is* a baby expected?"

Louise jerked her head to stare at Grant:

first indignant, then almost hysterically amused. Somehow this seemed the last straw. *"A baby?"* She buried her face in his neck and laughed and laughed.

But Grant's mind had swung to Marian Taylor. Had she listened to some rumour? Or deliberately lied? He very much suspected the latter. "I'm sorry . . ." Though relieved, he felt covered with confusion. "I've really dropped a clanger, this time."

"*You* haven't," Louise said, "but maybe someone else did. No, of course there's no baby on the way, Grant. Did Mrs Pryce think there might be?"

"No — not Mrs Pryce. Let's go back to that, later . . ." This was Marian's doing, he thought. Her bungalow was quite close to the Pryce's, so of course she knew these people. And if, in the course of visiting Eleanor, she had happened to spot Pryce at the annexe — then, knowing he was married gave her the chance to start off a whole chain of trouble.

Grant paused, releasing Louise from his arms as he gave himself up to serious thinking. He knew why Marian had acted as she had; only she wasn't quite as smart as she had thought. Her lie about the baby was an act of spite designed to put himself off Louise; and the letter Hilary Pryce had received must also have been her work. No doubt her purpose was to separate the Pryces — so that Adrian felt obliged to marry Louise? And with Grant put off Louise, Marian would feel she had a double chance. Grant wasn't conceited, for hadn't Marian made her intentions quite clear? He turned back to Louise, feeling grim.

"Did Marian ever see you with this fellow? Pryce, I mean," he said.

Louise blinked at the question. "I only know of one occsaion."

"Well, once would be enough," Grant said. "By the way, did you know he lives at Linsell Green, only a few doors from Marian's bungalow? No? Well, if you think about it, Louise, you don't need to be a sleuth to deduce who it was sent that letter."

"Surely not?" Yet Louise wasn't really surprised. That evening when Eleanor and Marian had seen Adrian bring her home, there had been something demoniac in Marian's expression; but at the time, it had seemed unimportant. Now, Louise found herself sharing Grant's suspicion. "She must hate me pretty badly," she said, aloud. "Don't tell me *she* said I was pregnant?"

"I'm afraid she did," he said, "but you have my word that I'll damn soon put a stop to that rumour. I'll scare the hide off Miss

Taylor! There'll be a letter in the post first thing tomorrow. You can take heart in one respect, Louise; I think the rumour about the baby went no further than myself; she was trying to put me off you," he said. Grant frowned. "She'd have a job to do that! However, may we shelve this topic for awhile? Right now, something's just come to me," he said.

As it had, for didn't Mrs Pryce say that letter was delivered by a girl with sandy hair? A girl with a dumpy figure? That description didn't fit Marian Taylor; but someone else had both of these characteristics — the girl now outside on the lawn.

Grant looked at Kim and decided he was right. "Who is that?" he asked.

"Kim Logan, the maid. What are we on to, now?" Louise queried.

"I'll tell you if I'm right," Grant said. "I think I'd like a few words with that lass. Ask her to come in, will you?"

"Oh, Grant, please — no! She's a little bit simple and easily scared," Louise protested. "I'm sure Kim hasn't done anything wrong."

"I'd still like her called in," Grant persisted. "I want to ask her a few questions. I shan't frighten her, at all; but that anonymous letter — she fits the description of the person who delivered it, and that is something I must find out."

"But she isn't *capable* of composing such a letter?"

"Maybe not, but she could push the finished product through a door, on someone else's instructions." Grant's blue-grey eyes still studied Kim. "Does she know Marian at all?"

"Well, she sees her when Marian calls on Eleanor."

"Thank you, that's all I want to know. Fetch her in, please."

Kim came willingly enough. "Was them respberries all right? And did you remember to rinse 'em first? They need plenty of sugar, too . . ." Then, noticing Grant, who was smiling at her: "Have I made a mistake? Did you mean me to come, now, or would you rather I ran back, later?"

Grant took over. "I'm a solicitor," he said, "and I'd like to ask you a question. Did anyone give you a sealed letter to put through the door of a bungalow at Linsell Green, last Monday?"

The girl jumped back as if he had hit her, but Grant went on, placidly indifferent: "It's important that you tell me, Kim. I promise you, you've nothing to fear. Just give me the truth, that's all."

Kim turned to Louise, trembling now. "Do I have to speak, Miss Mackenzie?"

"You don't *have* to, but I think it's better if you do." Sorry for the girl, Louise put an arm around her shoulder. "It doesn't mean you're going to get into trouble," she said. "But Mr Sullivan does have to know about this letter, and you're the only one who can help him."

"It won't mean no police?"

"Gracious, no!" Louise gave the girl a small squeeze. "Surely, you can trust me if I say it's all right Kim? Not to worry — Mr Sullivan is very kind; everyone knows that," she said.

Did Grant's eyes twinkle? Louise thought they did, but his attention went back to the shivering Kim. "Why are you afraid of me?" he coaxed.

"I ain't afraid," Kim said, quietly. "Not if Miss Mackenzie says it's all right. The only thing is —" Still trembling, she halted.

"Someone said you weren't to say?"

Kim nodded. "Well, I would like to help, honest I would, only I promised Miss Taylor I'd keep me mouth shut," she mumbled. Then: "Oh, *what* have I done?" The girl was verging on tears, now. "She's going to be so angry, I know she is! I've broken me word, now, haven't I?"

Grant leaned forward, smiling, to pat Kim's shoulder. "Sometimes, one has to break one's word," he said. "Miss Taylor was very wrong to bring you into this, but you don't have to worry any more. I doubt you will see her again, Kim."

Encouraged by Grant's manner, Kim volunteered: "I know it was on Monday, because Monday was me birthday, and Miss Taylor give me a lift. We stopped near a bungalow what had a yellow door, and that's where I delivered the letter. Miss Taylor also give me a lot of money," Kim explained, more to Louise than to Grant. "That's how I come to buy so much. But I've been worried, since — about the letter, I mean. I didn't like the way that envelope was addressed. All them letters stuck on!"

"Well, you can forget the whole business, now," Grant said.

"Except I broke me word . . ."

Louise laughed. "No, everything's fine," she said. "And by the way, those raspberries were gorgeous!" She slipped the girl a pound. "Keep smiling," she said, "and thank you for helping us, Kim."

Grant remarked, as the girl lumbered back to Robins Rest: "This calls for a second letter, Louise . . . one I'll really enjoy writing! I take it," he quirked an eyebrow at her, "that you won't want to bring a case against Marian for defamation of character, and so on? I'd suggest a warning letter would be quite sufficient."

"Then if you write, can we leave it at that?" Louise asked. She added, feeling suddenly shy: "Thank you for seeing to all this for me. I'm more grateful than you know; but how does one say so?"

"You don't *say* it . . ." Grant hauled her back into his arms. "There are more ways than one in which to thank a person. By the way, why the hell am I troubling, Miss Mackenzie? Aren't you the girl who sent me packing?"

Nineteen

Several kisses later, Louise enquired: "So have we now finished all discussions?"

"Well, we can tie any loose ends up, later." Grant said. "Shall we forget the Pryces and Marian, and keep the rest of the day for ourselves? A nice idea would be to go out to lunch. There's a good hotel not far along the road. How does that appeal?"

"Very nice . . ." Like old times! Louise thought.

"By the way," he said, "where is Eleanor Russell? Do you realise I haven't linked up with her, yet? Has she emigrated, or something?"

"She's spending the weekend with Mother and Bernard. Just as well!" Louise said, bubbling laughter. "I'm very fond of Eleanor, but there are occasions —" She left the sentence unfinished and sighed.

Grant exploded into chuckles. "Exactly!" he said. "Still an avid talker, is she?" He kissed Louise and sent her blood racing. "We'll have to see if *we* can give her some news to spread around! Nice news, I mean . . ."

The girl made no comment: only met Grant's eyes and gave him a slow gentle smile. She wasn't going to jump too soon to conclusions; for all she knew, she had misunderstood him, and could even embarrass him, she thought.

As for Grant, his mind did a quick unroll: spared a moment to ask Annabel's blessing, knowing she would want him to be happy. He saw himself as a lucky man; for had he not been fortunate, he asked himself, in knowing these two lovely girls? The one, a memory he would treasure forever: the other, a loving promise for the future.

He was glad when Louise broke the silence by saying: "That's the church clock striking twelve. Did somebody mention lunch?"

"I did — and lunch was what I said, not supper; so we'd better get a move on," he said. "Incidentally," his eyes seemed to hold her own, "we've gone full cycle, now, Louise. We began with a meal, before, remember? Don't let's act like fools a second time . . ."

Again, she said nothing. It wasn't the moment to bring their new acquaintance to its final stage; but she could not resist leaving a kiss on Grant's cheek before hurrying away to her bedroom. Having looked through her dresses, she chose her favourite: a very feminine model in a cool cream, patterned with splashes of flowers. She gave her hair a few quick strokes of the brush, touched her mouth with lipstick, then went through to join Grant, again.

"Ready so soon? That's my girl!" he laughed. "No keeping her man waiting an hour . . . and you really look a million," he told her. They locked the annexe and set off along the drive, just in time to wave to the elderly vicar who had called to collect Kim Logan.

"She's friendly with the maid at the vicarage," Louise explained, "as Eleanor is away, they've invited Kim to lunch, which is a good thing, Grant — it will take her mind off that letter."

"Yes, it will . . ." Grant acknowledged the vicar's salute. "Someone else to whom we can give some nice news! And on that subject," he said, smiling at Louise, "let's make it soon . . . *very soon!*" She looked at him and saw with sudden joy that happiness had wiped all grief from his eyes; that he was ready to love, ready to be loved, again . . .

She couldn't believe it was she who'd wrought this change; yet Grant's smile, speaking for his heart, just then, told her very plainly that he loved her. She felt touched by the magic of it all.

And what he'd said was true, she thought: they'd be fools, indeed, if they let this second chance slip through their hands. Love was too precious to squander. Besides, they knew so well, now, that they belonged to each other; knew that no other love could match this one that would hold them together, always.

At her side, Grant reached for Louise's nearest hand. "You know that hardened bachelor girl?" he said. "The one who was never going to marry — not she! She had too much sense — remember? Well, isn't it a good thing I've come back in time to rescue her from such an awful fate?"

She laughed. "Yes, Grant, it's a very good thing! The best that's ever happened to her, I'd say . . ." His kisses, long and searching, halted her words; but as he'd said, there'd be time to talk, later.

We hope you have enjoyed this Large Print book. Other Thorndike, Wheeler, and Chivers Press Large Print books are available at your library or directly from the publishers.

For information about current and upcoming titles, please call or write, without obligation, to:

Publisher
Thorndike Press
295 Kennedy Memorial Drive
Waterville, ME 04901
Tel. (800) 223-1244

or visit our Web site at:

www.gale.com/thorndike
www.gale.com/wheeler

OR

Chivers Large Print
published by BBC Audiobooks Ltd
St James House, The Square
Lower Bristol Road
Bath BA2 3SB
England
Tel. +44(0) 800 136919
email: bbcaudiobooks@bbc.co.uk
www.bbcaudiobooks.co.uk

All our Large Print titles are designed for easy reading, and all our books are made to last.